Nevertheless

Unravelling The Mystery

Gulsar Almash

Ukiyoto Publishing

All global publishing rights are held by

Ukiyoto Publishing

Published in 2023

Content Copyright © Gulsar Almash

ISBN 9789360165574

All rights reserved.

No part of this publication may be reproduced, transmitted, or stored in a retrieval system, in any form by any means, electronic, mechanical, photocopying, recording or otherwise, without the prior permission of the publisher.

The moral rights of the author have been asserted.

This is a work of fiction. Names, characters, businesses, places, events, locales, and incidents are either the products of the author's imagination or used in a fictitious manner. Any resemblance to actual persons, living or dead, or actual events is purely coincidental.

This book is sold subject to the condition that it shall not by way of trade or otherwise, be lent, resold, hired out or otherwise circulated, without the publisher's prior consent, in any form of binding or cover other than that in which it is published.

www.ukiyoto.com

To those having faith on fate.
If it's destined to be yours, it'll be.

Acknowledgement

Thank you god for everything. I'd want to offer my heartfelt gratitude to everyone who helped make this book a reality. This endeavour would not have been feasible without their guidance, insight, and encouragement.

First and foremost, I'd like to thank my Sisters, and My friend Mounika for their constant support and belief in me during this journey. Your support and encouragement laid the groundwork for this book.

I am also grateful to my Advisor, whose knowledge and counsel helped define the course of this work. Your helpful thoughts and constructive suggestions were critical in helping me refine my ideas. I'd like to thank the editors who generously offered their time, skills, and resources. Your contributions improved the breadth and depth of this work.

Thank you all for being a part of this journey. I am eternally grateful for your help and support.

With love,
Gulsar Almash

Playlist

Your Love – Jim Brickman
My Love – Westlife
Destiny – Jim Brickman
You Are My Everything – Gummy
Nothing' Going to Change – Westlife
Somewhere Only We Know – Keane
Take Me to Your Heart – Michael Learns to Rock
Breaking Down – AILEE
Dynasty – MIIA
Song of the Wind – PIVOVAROV, Khrystyna Soloviy

https://open.spotify.com/playlist/2oxKEy6OZMSg69N1MjPnAM?si=Q6ecNaxGQ-mHK30Vb6YlnA

Contents

Part One	1
One Aera	3
Two Bong-Cha	10
Three Aera	20
Four Bong-Cha	27
Five Aera	34
Six Aera	41
Seven Aera	48
Eight Bong-Cha	54
Nine Aera	61
Ten Bong-Cha	67
Eleven Aera	73
Twelve Bong-Cha	81
Thirteen Bong-Cha	87
Fourteen Bong-Cha	93
Fifteen Aera	99
Sixteen Aera	106
Seventeen Aera	115
Eighteen Aera	122
Nineteen Bong-Cha	128
Twenty Aera	136
Part Two	141
Twenty One Kim-Woo	143
Twenty Two Kim-Woo	150
Twenty Three Kim-Woo	155
Twenty Four Kim-Woo	161
Twenty Five Kim-Woo	167
Twenty Six Aera	170
Twenty Seven Bong-Cha	178
Epilogue Kim-Woo	183
About the Author	*187*

Part One

Nevertheless

One
Aera

Everybody in daily life has a specific task to complete. Busan is a bustling metropolis with a large population. A beautiful meadow in summer or spring with two fluttering butterflies and forget-me-not blue flowers. The wild natural setting from an aerial top-down perspective of a beach with a blue ocean, white-capped waves, and beautiful sand.

We rush to complete all our tasks on a busy day. Bong-cha is preoccupied with her makeup, Dalia with her breakfast, and I am with the vessels. I'm Park-Shin, and I've been Aera for as long as anyone can remember. We have been living together as roommates for nearly three years. We are rushing to finish everything before 8:00 a.m. because if we don't, we'll miss our bus. Gaze set on the clock; I ask my friends to complete everything quickly.

We are late as usual. The driver begins blowing the horn, which sounds like the Grim Reaper's last call. We hurry to catch the bus. Dalia's next breath is shallow; barely any oxygen reaches its destination. But we couldn't blame her lungs or brain for being sluggish all the time.

But Bong-cha refuses to give up. She begins to run as if she's in a race with Usain Bolt; she's the coolest among us. The fearless one. She gets on another bus and calls us. I pull myself together enough to gather my energy. I pull Dalia's hand and start running towards the bus.

We eventually made it inside, and I sat down to rest. I'm exhausted; it's as if my heart is beating inside my head. I'm feeling dizzy. Even though we always miss our bus, we have never rushed or chased after one.

My phone pings with a notification. That sharp and loud sound breaks the silence and jolts me out of my trance.

'Where you guys are?'

'Don't tell me you're late as usual'

Our instructor texted me to make it quick. I left her without replying.

"Crap, why is the bus moving so slowly today?"

My eyelids fall shut. Silence begins to spread, and suddenly, there is a big bang. I open one eye, taking a peek at where my friends are. Bong-cha informs me that we have reached this place. I wipe my sleepy face with tissues, use compact powder, and apply my red velvet tint to my lips. I head towards the doorway of the bus.

When we get off the bus, there are several other school buses nearby. I feel like I've gotten myself into a herd of bulls. I did not see a single student apart from our classmates and instructors. They are all furious at us. They are about to burn us with their gaze.

"We're waiting because of you three," our tutor yells. She turns on the advice radio. I expect a new topic this time, but it is about punctuality, which we lack.

Ha…. It's common, and we're used to it.

"All right, let's get inside… It's getting late again," he utters in his deep voice. Hyun-Bin, this man is the one I secretly crush on. The only person who can make my heart flutter. It's him; I hear myself murmuring as I stare at him. He comes closer, and my heart skips a beat for him. It's him—the one who occupies my whole gallery. My secret photos of him and his cool and somehow cute demeanour

"You look even cooler now." shit, what am I doing? I clasp my mouth shut, feeling an intense blush on my cheeks.

"Don't be late again," he says as he approaches closer and passes a crispy smile by waving his eyebrows.

"Hold on. That means_____

He's talking to me!"

No. No way, how? Is this a dream? This could never happen. But then he says, "I know you, Aera; I'm a huge fan of your radio podcasting." He continues, "I never missed it."

The blush spread to the tips of my ears, and I imagined the ground beneath me opening up and swallowing me right now. Something I realise now is that I'm not so unlucky.

I can't be so fortunate. But it is true. I have a feeling it is. And luck, destiny, fate, and whatever else decides this moment of mine have done me a great favor. I believe in cupid for the first time. Perhaps the cupid fired an arrow that stabbed him today.

The instructor double-checked our attendance and gave us a little general information about the venue. She then handed out our passes. We head over there.

I'm bored just getting in; I don't like such places. But I remember going there as a kid. My face shrank when we got inside. Boys and girls have separate lines. I desperately want to accompany Hyun-Bin Oppa, but he is in the boy's line.

It's just me and him. Oh, my God, it's so romantic. I persuade myself. But it's enough to know that he knows who I am and enjoys my podcast. I'll just stay here and keep an eye on him over there.

"Hello...Aera," a husky chorus voice approaches from the direction of Hyun-Bin. They rush over to me, hug me tightly, and greet me with those obligatory cheek kisses.

"Damn, how did I forget about them?"

Years ago, when I was at my university, I felt some trepidation because it was my first day in a new city with new people. I walked through the gate and inside. Some welcomed me with a smile, while others bullied me. I rush down the corridor, embarrassed.

Someone suddenly grabbed my hand. I'm scared, but I don't show it, and I ask with a strange reaction by waving my eyebrows up.

"Who are you?"

"We two are new here, just like you. Don't be scared. My name is Yang-Min, and my boyfriend's name is Hyun-Yang."

Boyfriend? I burst out laughing. "Do you know each other previously?"

"Yeah, we've been friends since we were kids. But now we're more than friends," they admitted, smiling sweetly.

I smiled at them and continued my conversation. I've only seen Bromance on TV shows. It's strange to see a new gay couple in real life. Anyway, they are cute, and I like them. They have shown the same love and affection since then.

What a cute couple. Angry Birds, Tom and Jerry, Jack and Jill, or any other cute names you can think of are perfect for them. The buzz on our campus Yang couple (Hyun-Yang and Yang-Min)—I have never seen a sweeter bromance. Lovely people with pure hearts.

"Aera, you're late as usual." They laugh and pat my shoulders. Hyun-Yang hands me Binggrae strawberry milk. One of my favourite milk drinks. I accept it, and we walk in together.

The Royal Museum will mark its 75th anniversary in the second week of September. They provide free visiting passes to all high schools and universities, allowing students to learn about Korean norms and history.

It's important to understand our country's history, but I'm not that kind of person. I don't spend a lot of time researching the past.

I mean_____

I respect that, but I am not that person. Therefore, today will be one of my most boring days. I suppose so.

Bong-Cha will probably enjoy this place. She will be more certain. Well, she has been a historophile since childhood. We have a lot of antiques in our room as well. She enjoys collecting. Her high school major is history, and she has a good grade point average.

I suppose she will explain everything here first, before the instructor.

Ha ha…

Everyone is too excited to analyse this place, except one person. You've probably guessed who. Yeah, I am. I move around like an ant in search of sweets. Bong-cha requests that I stay close to her and not go anywhere alone. She's sick of worrying about me; perhaps she thinks I'm reckless.

The museum has developed significantly since its inception. This time commemorate the occasion by filling the museum with exhibits about the great 'Silla'.

Silla is an ancient Korean kingdom. Before the Korean War, the country was divided into three kingdoms: Baekji, Silla, and Goguryeo.

Does it sound appealing? All the historical facts I knew were taught to me by Bong-Cha. She can most likely explain better than I can.

Two
Bong-Cha

"I am looking for Aera. Where has she gone?"

"Move, move, I'm here...." she says as she approaches me. It's hard for me to forget the first time I met Aera. I've known her since I was a child. When I returned to Korea, I ran into her at this museum. I identify as a Korean American. When I was a kid, my parents lived in the United States. Following the birth of my brother, we relocated to Korea.

In the United States, my father worked in an auction house. He frequently discusses American history. My father sparked my interest in history.

Once I dug in our backyard and discovered a coin. I handed it to my father, who explained that it was an antique. We sold it at his workplace auction house. This incident piqued my curiosity and interest in history. I've been collecting antiques since then, and I'm really into it.

My father took me to this museum when we returned to Korea. That was my first visit to a museum in Korea. In historical terms, Korean history drove me insane.

I noticed a girl with enormous eyes wearing a lovely gown sobbing in front of a statue. I drew closer and approached her.

"What happened? Are you all right?" I inquired, with concern.

"I came here with my father, and I missed him. What do I do now?" she mumbled. I called my father, and told him this, and he went up to the museum's security to make a statement about this little girl.

We waited for a while before her father entered the security room. He ran and cried, hugging his daughter. Finally, I discovered that she had inherited her father's large, attractive eyes. He thanked us and the security guards before leaving with his daughter.

After graduating from high school, I enrolled at the Silla University of Arts. On the first day of college, I noticed a girl walking awkwardly down the corridor. I got the same vibe as I did in the museum when I was five. I approached to speak to her, but she was interrupted, and I lost her. Later, I went home and talked about that girl for hours, despite only seeing her for a few minutes.

Sounds crazy, right? Let me continue.

Then I moved away from my family and rented a room for myself. There were two, and I shared my flat with them. I can't believe what I'm seeing. I found her_____

I finally found her; I approached her first and initiated the conversation. Aera and Dalia introduced themselves. We talked a lot and became very close within a few hours. I shared about myself and my interests. My passion for history and collecting antiques. Then, Aera shared some childhood photos of herself, and I realized that the girl I saw earlier at the museum was Aera. But she had forgotten about it. That's how Aera and Dalia became my friends.

"Why are you staring at me?" Aera questions, raising her brows.

"Um_____ Nothing,

Just some memories of us popped into my mind."

"Stop thinking about old memories,

Let's make some new ones.

Let's go____" Aera says, taking my hands, and begins to walk through the crowd.

The Royal Museum was drastically transformed. It appears more developed than before. I recall every word my father talked to me about this museum. It's all about history, pride, and so on. I'm not sure how my father knows so much about Korean history, but I'm learning more about Korea and its norms and culture.

But there are a lot of antiques here that I have not seen before. It makes me want to discover more, but this time it's about Silla.

"Aera, take a look at this armor; it was worn by a great Goguryeo soldier during the 16th-century war. This armor is made of iron and protects them from arrows and other weapons of their rivals," I explain, but she gives me a strange look.

"Do you know why we use chopsticks?" When I press her further, she drops my hands and runs over to Dalia, hiding behind her.

"Why is she running away?

I just explained it to her; did I bore her?" I know she's not interested in history, but not this much.

I take my time approaching all the exhibits in the museum. My eyes begin to scan every element. And I am drawn to a sword on the left side of mine. It's completely enclosed and kept in a safety locker. And no one is allowed to get too close to the sword. It piqued my interest, so I read the details in the bottom right corner of the showpiece.

"General Kim-Woo's sword?" I exclaim, having never heard this name before. This makes me feel as if I haven't learned enough about Silla.

"Yes, this sword was used by General Kim-Woo," a deep and warm voice approaches. I am startled to hear this voice. I eventually turn slowly and see that person's eyes.

A tall man, almost 5'7, with broad shoulders, dark brown eyes, and a typical handsome Korean face, but slightly old. Stood face to face and stared at me.

"Who are you? You almost scared me" I enquire and face him eventually.

"Um_____

Well, I'm a traveler," he says, staring at the sword.

I think he is new to this place. I am surprised to see such a man. His appearance, style, and even slang are distinctive. He's rolling his eyes more frequently and appears allergic to crowds.

"What exactly are you doing here?" Why I asking such a stupid question? What do most people do in museums?

"I'm sorry, can you elaborate?" I ask him.

"This sword was made of carbon steel, with a single-edged curved blade and typically a wood grip. Along with a sword guard."

"Does this belong to you? How do you know these specifics? Are you a historian?" I barrage him with questions.

"Why don't you give me a chance to explain?" He launches a counter-attack and smile at me.

"Heck"

I pat my back head and begin listening. I focus my complete attention on his mouth.

"No, no, no....." I'm going to see his eye this time because his pink lips distracts me.

"Kim-Woo does not own this sword. He received this sword as a token of honor. This sword was made for a great Silla warrior who faced many rivals and had drenched in the blood of Silla's greedy enemies."

"Wait, who is the noble warrior?"

"Are you aware of that?" I'm powerless to stop myself. My pupils enlarge as I widen my eyes and activate my brain.

"This sword belongs to Yoon-Woo, Kim-Woo's father. Kim-woo was as enraged and courageous as his father. They both served as Silla's general and_____"

"And, what? Please tell me" I ask him to go on.

I get goosebumps, my hair stiffens, and I hear a voice calling me repeatedly, but it is unclear. It appears too far away for me. It repeats, but this time in a chorus. I try to figure it out, but I can't hear any further or see who is calling. Suddenly, a hand behind me grabs my shoulders.

Boo......

After a deep breath, my lungs let go of the air they were holding, and I became conscious. It's as if I've stepped into another world. I turn slowly, my heart rate increases, and it is our tutor.

"You terrify me," I say, and I still can't stop panicking. It accelerates; I can feel my heartbeat on my wrist.

"Are you alright?" My tutor inquires. She pampers me and pat my back slowly. She eventually called my friends and ask them to bring me to the first aid room. I have phonophobia, which is a persistent, abnormal, and unjustified fear of sound. It frequently approaches in the form of normal environmental sounds such as traffic, crowds, loud speech, and even sudden door closing.

I get my first aid and return to my friends, but this time the tutor asks me to stay within her sight.

It's kinda annoying, but I've got to so, I follow her. I could hear footsteps approaching. "The tutor asks us to stay with you," say the cute Yang couple. "By the way, are you alright now?"

"It's a lot better than before. Because of my phonophobia, this happens frequently. I'm used to it," I say with a bitter smile because I still feel dizzy.

"Are you able to walk?" Hyun-Yang inquire, slightly biting his lips.

"I can." I stretch my shoulders and return to my exploration. Yang-Min approach his hands and extend his earmuffs to me.

"Because I usually nap while traveling, I always bring earmuffs and an eye mask. It's for avoiding noise and other things." He hands it to me, his veiny hands capturing my attention.

What happened to me? Why are these guys attracting me today? I murmur and accept it.

"Aw..., you're so sweet, I really need it." We begin to walk after I respond. I start the conversation, and now

I'm back to my old self. I begin talking about Silla, and these people are far better than Aera. At the very least, they are responding to me.

"Silla? This is something I have heard before." Hyun-Yang steps in.

"Yeah, maybe in high school history classes." I raise my brows and fire at him with my sharp nose.

"I've got it. Yang, it's from the Hwarang drama. Don't you recall that?" Yang-Min exclaims joyfully.

Finally, everyone remembered Silla. It's not so much about Silla as it is about Hwarang. It's a 2016 Korean television series with a global audience. The large cast, and my bias, Kim-Taehyung, played a charming character in the drama.

The conversation progresses, and we talk a lot. It's a lot of fun with them. These cuties away took all of my anxiety and stress. There is no doubt about why these two are known as our university cuties.

I notice Dalia standing alone near our tutor and conversing with her, and then I remember Aera. I couldn't see her in the sea of students and people. Where has she vanished? It took me by surprise. She's the most careless person I've ever seen, and she's prone to getting lost. I am constantly concerned about her actions.

"Is she going to the restroom or somewhere else?" I mumble to myself and approach Dalia to inquire.

"She went to the first-aid room to look for you." Listening to this made me nervous. Aera had been lost in this place before, which is why she despises museums. And she's still a child who is easily duped by anyone. I must notify our instructor. I inform her, and she asks that we divide into groups and search for Aera. We go looking for her along with our classmates.

I call her name as my eyes begin to scan the crowd. "Where have you gone, Aera?"

In a mass of students, it is difficult to spot a short girl with black hair. My mind is exhausting, and my heart is aching; where has she gone? It kept happening inside of me. I will never forget the day she burst into tears in front of me. I will never let her cry again. She's my friend, and I can go to any length for her. I take off my earmuff and start looking. I ran to the parking lot, hoping to find her sleeping there.

When I get on our bus, it is empty. "Did you happen to see Aera?" I ask the bus driver, who replies with a nod from right to left. He approached again to ask a question, but I had already exit. I inquire of the students whether they have found her. But I received a big No.....

"How about going to the Art Gallery? (The painting section). I'm sure she'll be there," Yang-Min interrupts.

"Sure, let's go there," our tutor summons all of our classmates and other students to the art gallery.

I approach first and look for her. I notice a shorty with black wavy hair standing in front of a painting, wearing a short skirt and a top.

"Park-Shin, I got you," I yell. Why is she not responding to me? I exclaim, my mind racing with questions.

Three
Aera

Something is strange; I have an excruciating pain in the back of my head, specifically in my medulla. I sit on the floor and closed my eyes. The pain is unbearable; my menstrual cycles are far better than this. I notice some illusions colliding inside my eyes, but nothing is clear. I crossed my legs and wrapped my arms around my body. My lungs are filling with oxygen, and the balloon is growing larger and larger. Holding my breath puts strain on my ribcage.

I cock my head and notice a painting to my right. I am hit by a spark. The air that had been trapped in my lungs is slowly being released. Those memories I saw in my illusion faded slowly, and I approach the painting cautiously. I am surprised to find myself drawn to an art. A painting, almost 4 meters in height and 8 meters in width. The art is painted on silk and framed with a wooden frame.

The art expresses the pain it contains and extends its impact to the viewers. The red colour had almost finished the painting. It depicts a poignant love story set in a war zone. On a battlefield, a javelin stabbed a couple while embracing. I can feel their anguish through the painting. The artist painted the girl's eye with such detail, expressing the anguish of love.

I approached the painting, and I don't know what was happening around me. I stare at the painting and feel the pain the girl experienced. I read the details of the painting. An ancient artist drew this drawing 'The Tear of Love'. It portrays the love story of General Kim-Woo and Shin-Min.

"Kim-Woo?" I blurted out strangely. Then I observed every detail mentioned by the artist in the painting. My entire focus is on the showpiece, and I feel as if I have entered the battle zone. It is Bong-Cha who approaches me from behind.

"Are you alright? We've been looking for you. What are you doing here?" she chastised.

I shrug my shoulders and redirect my attention to the painting. I avoid making eye contact with Bong-Cha. Wiggling my toes inside my socks and not keeping my gaze on her.

Our instructor and classmates have arrived at the location. Fear causes my heart to beat quickly. Our instructor is a hundred times worse than Bong-Cha when it comes to scolding. Today is likely my last day. "Aera, rest in peace," I mutter to myself as I face my tutor.

"I'm sorry, madam," I say, a small and bitter smile on my face. My instructor is as angry as the sun, but it is my fault. I troubled my tutor and made my friends search for me everywhere.

She unexpectedly hugged and patted me on the back. My mother always gives me a warm, whole-body hug, it's been few months since I got one. After that, I hadn't received a hug like this in a long time. I feel better after the hug that our tutor offered. I had never seen our instructor do anything like this before. Later, a friendly voice approaches, "Are you alright?"

"Um..." I opened my mouth to respond to her, but nothing comes out. Bong-Cha clenched her fists and awkwardly stepped in front of me.

"Hey, look, I'm fine," I say as I lift her hands.

"Thank you for looking for me," I add.

"Friends don't do things expecting thanks," she confesses as she hugs me. Dalia joins us.

"Enough, guys, I can't let the oxygen out," Dalia yells, and we laugh as we release her.

"Let's return to the bus because we're already running late. We need to get back to the university as soon as possible," our instructor interrupted, summoning us to the parking lot.

"Mrs Park, please excuse my interruption."

"Could you explain this artwork?" I ask, biting my lower lip and giving her a cute expression.

"Why this one?" she inquired, flipping through the pages of a book she is holding. Her eyes roll, and her fingers flip as quickly as they can.

"I got them...."

"Ah, this painting belongs to the 16th-century Silla. The Tear of Love, painted by the great artist Ban-Ru, depicts the love story of his friends Kim-Woo and Shin-Min. The story revolves around two lovers who have high expectations for their relationship. But the war dashed all of their hopes," she continues.

"They gave their lives for Silla. After defeating the rival nation's king, all of his soldiers fled and escaped. Kim-Woo rushed over to Shin-Min, embracing her tightly in his arms like a warm blanket enveloping a cold person. But then a javelin was thrust into them. It's heart breaking to hear that they collapsed and died while hugging each other."

Tears are welling up in everyone's eyes. My eyes are tearing up uncontrollably. Even though I try to stop crying, I fail.

"This is terrible; it should not have happened," the Yangs sobbed. I turn and re-watch the art; I still believe it contains some mystery, and I want to know the entire tale of this couple.

A lot of questions arises within me, such as why I am drawn to this? Why I am suddenly experiencing a lot of unrelated illusions? And what is the full story behind this? I board the bus, with questions filling my mind.

Bong-Cha sits with Dalia on the left side, while I sit alone on the right. I sit by myself to take a nap because I am exhausted. Bong-Cha and Dalia asked if I was okay. I responded and eventually closed my eyes. Someone is sitting by my side, but I don't look to see who it is. Maybe it's one of my friend.

I gradually fall asleep. My brain relaxes, and I feel a sense of relief.

Wait_____

What am I hearing? It's a familiar male voice. I think I'm used to it. I try, but I cannot guess who it is. You can try again, Aera. I activate my brain and make it as effective as possible. My nerves and brain works, and I'm almost there.

"Yeah, I got em.

I've got you, Hyun-Bin." I stood up and burst out shouting. Oh no, what did I did? I mumble as I raise my head. I'm not sure why I screamed at such an embarrassing moment. I used to despise our driver, but not anymore. He abruptly pulls the brake, and I fall down.

Ah, um…. No, it's not quite down. I landed on Hyun-Bin's lap. He carries me in his arms with care. His right arm lifting my hip, while his left arm holds my head. I feel safe and at ease around him. His adorable eyes and lips, I can't help but fall for him. I wish to make eye contact with him for a while, but my friend Dalia, that idiot, interrupts me.

"Are you alright, Aera?" she inquires with care.

"Well, yeah, I'm alright," I reply, but I am not.

I will never get another chance to get close to him. I'm going to confront this person.

"Daliaaaa…" I mutter through clenched teeth.

"Hey, Hyun-Bin, are okay? And I sincerely apologize."

"That's fine, you're not that heavy," he laughs.

I shrug my shoulders and smile faintly, the smallest smile I've ever mustered. Hyun-Bin went back and sat with his friends.

Bong-Cha, move over to my side. She sits beside me. She takes the left ear bud from my ear and places it into her left ear. That's her favourite song, "Stay with Me" from the K-Drama Goblin. She enjoys fiction and believes in fate. She even believes that people have three lives.

"What happened to you previously at the museum?"

"What?" I ask as I pause the song.

"Did you say anything?"

"Can you tell me what happened at the museum?" she repeats.

"Well, I'm not sure. I became bored and started wandering around. Then I noticed the painting that attracted me. As I got closer, I saw a couple kissing and hugging. Suddenly, they both collapsed and..."

"What happened?"

"I'm not sure; I just saw some teary eyes closing and then....."

"Aera, I saw you crying in front of the painting and wondered why. What is it about that specific painting that captivates you? There's something fishy going on."

"There's nothing fishy about it, Bong-Cha. It simply drew me in. And those visions could just be my imagination. Perhaps I overheard it somewhere and remembered it. But I'm curious about the true story of the couple. I wish to know the whole story"

"How do we know that, though?" she let out a sigh.

Time can change history, but it can't change love. In both my vision and the painting, I felt a profound and intense love. The pain of love is evident in the girl's eyes. I sensed something deep and loving in those eyes.

When arrived at our university, they asked us to disembark out, and we did so one by one.

"Dalia, where are you?"

"Wait, I'll check," Yang-Min says as he goes inside and playfully yells my name.

I, Bong-Cha, and a few of our friends board the bus. Yang-Min is taking photographs near the back seat. He asks so that we approached quietly. Oh, my eyes! What on earth am I seeing? Does a 20-year-old do these things while sleeping?

"Dalia, Dalia..." Bong-Cha tries to wake her up.

"Leave me alone, I'm tired," she groan as she rolls.

Bang!!!

"Ouch, where am I?"

"Not in your bedroom, lady," Yang-Min teases, and we burst out laughing. I lift my helpless baby Dalia and assist her in getting off the bus.

Four
Bong-Cha

What's going on? I question myself sceptically. When my friends and I walked in, everyone is staring at us. They're making fun of us. Some people were pointing at Dalia and laughing at her while staring at their phones. Finally, I received an explanation: it was all because of Dalia's sleeping photo. Yang-Min posted a photo of herself in our institute's student group. It's a large group with many members on KakaoTalk.

I noticed some posters of Dalia sucking her fingers as we passed through the corridor. Omo, Dalia gets mad and dashes into our classroom. There is a large poster of her in the room. Yang-Min yells, "Sleeping baby, sleeping baby...."

And this infuriates her. Dalia rips up the poster and yells his name. He has multiple posters. He takes one and begins dancing in front of everyone. Dalia dashes forward and jumps on Yang-Min. She hits him on the back while sitting on his back like a piggyback. He grabbed her tightly on his shoulder. Hyun-Yang became envious, but he knew it is only to mock Dalia. He sat Dalia on his back and rides her around our campus.

"Look who is coming. It's our sleeping cry baby," he shouts.

"Let me go!" Dalia shouts back. As usual, they're quarrelling.

Yang-Min used to make fun of Dalia all the time, but that is no longer the case. Dalia became enraged and launched her attack. She has some pictures of the Yangs that are too personal. She posted them on KakaoTalk. It exacerbates the fight, and they both sit down and decide to talk about it. Aera and Hyun-Yang persuades them. But they aren't done yet. They relocated to continue this in a new location, lol. Aera and Hyun-Yang accompany them.

Because I dislike fighting and prefer peace, I start walking to my seat. I slipped after colliding with something unexpected. I fell and almost hit the ground, but I couldn't feel it. I burst out in surprise.

"I but_____

Why didn't my head or body fall to the ground?"

"Because you're on top of me and I'm on the ground, you're not feeling it, only I am."

Is this Hyun-Bin? I stood up and extended my hand to help him stand. He's smiling at me, I've noticed it. He grabs my hands and steps forward. We're standing close together, so close that our noses are touching. He is still holding my hands and won't let go. I turn to face him and lift my head.

His eyes, those captivating eyes, are fixed on mine, and then they shifted to my lips. He gets too close to me, and the small distance between us diminishes. I squeeze my eyes shut and close them. It feels like heaven when he touches my face and brushes my cheeks. After a brief pause, he picked an eyelash from my cheek. He grabs my hands and places the eyelash on my palm as I open my eyes.

"Make a wish," he says.

"What?" I'm perplexed.

"Make a wish and blow the lash, and your wish will come true," he stated with a smile. I remain silent without uttering a word.

He closes his eyes and blow the lash on my hand in a split second. My heart is melting from the warm breath escaping his mouth. My heart rate was increasing, and I could hear them in my head.

So, I smile and move away from him. I dash to the restroom, leaving my backpack behind. My cheeks had turned red, and I was afraid he would notice. Why am I still having feelings for Hyun-Bin?

Love is a powerful force that can be difficult to control.

My childhood neighbour was Hyun-Bin. We walked hands in hands through the children's park, both of us in love. It was my first experience of puppy love and my first true love. His family later moved to a new apartment, and he stopped visiting me. He did not know that I was the girl he once loved. But I remember him, and I haven't forgotten about him. I still love him, but how dare I approach him after all these years? All our promises are nothing but silly childhood memories. Soon, I will have to forget about all of them and move on.

I wipe my face with tissues after dampening them with water. When I step outside and tilt my head to the right, I realize I am almost late for my first class. So, I sped up and hit someone. He trips and falls. I extend my hand to assist him in getting up. It's been two minutes, but he still hasn't grabbed my hands yet.

"Don't you want to get up?" I spit out as he refuses to grab my hands. What? Nobody had ever refused me before. Who is he? How could he refuse me? No one had ever done anything like this before... literally no one.

He stands up and begins walking. The sounds of his footsteps echoed throughout the campus. My eyes widen as I see such a magnificent walk.

"Wait," I shout.

He paused and slowly turns to face me. I can't believe what I'm seeing. He's here!!! It is a miracle. I finally met you. He gives a sweet smile. And I'm still frozen; I assume I'll never see him again.

"Do you remember me?" he asks, his deep, warm voice reaching my ears. He approaches me, and I stand still in shock.

"Hey, Miss"

"Ah_____ yes, yes, I remember you. How do you think I'll forget about you? And are you hurt? I'm sorry I hit on you. What are you doing here, man?"

"Wait...... miss you didn't even change. You're always bombarding me with questions."

"How will I change in a single day?" I'm still wondering what this man is doing here. I inquire, and he pause for a moment. Then he reveals he is our new librarian. Oh, what a blessing to have such a gifted man as our librarian. I mean, he knows everything there is to know about history and classics. He's perfect for this profession. I apologized and told him that, I'd come to see him in my free time at the library. He didn't say much and he just smiles. I greet him by bowing my head.

How did I forget this? crap_____

I'm running late? I hurried to class.

When I arrive at the classroom, I could still hear some noise, screams, and shouts, showing that the teacher is not present. I enter, waving my hands and tapping my foot firmly on the floor. He's standing right there! I notice Hyun-Bin standing in front of me. I'm blushing again because I'm embarrassed. No, Bong-Cha! Never again. I could see his gaze in his eyes, but I didn't allow him to meet my gaze this time.

Dalia calls out my name, so I went there. They're still arguing about what they did. Aera is having fun with the fight.

Aera yells, "Stop it!" when I arrive. Suddenly, I feel a pleasant silence there. I know she did it for me because I'm sensitive to noise. She grabs my hands in hers and direct me to our places.

"What happens to you? You moron. I'm afraid; please notify me before going anywhere, understand?"

"I just went to the restroom, and look at me, Tada." I try to make her laugh, but she refused. I know we both are concern with each other, though I am not a kid, who doesn't even know to go to the washroom alone. How damn I tell this to her. She hands me my earmuffs and tells me to take them with me wherever I go.

"I'll hang out with you if you're a guy." I look her into her eyes. She takes my face in her hands and approaches me. "You can even date me now, you lil girl, as the Yang couples do," she whispers when she reach my ears. I burst out laughing and I say, "I am a lesbian for you Aera, lol." We laugh hard.

Not everyone is fortunate to have their first love; it is hard to keep it forever and even more difficult to forget. A memory filled with silly conversations, unreasonable fights, a secret relationship, and cute gifts. I wish I could reclaim him. I want him to hold my hands again, pat my head, and buy me candy. I wish I could redo everything.

My eyes became red, so I lean back in my chair and take my backpack. I take my purse and unzip it. I take a letter I had previously written. It appears to be old, and those letters have been smudged and spread. I wrote it when we were young. Because I am a bit bossy, I express myself less. This was the first thing I did to show my affection for him. I didn't get to give this to him. Before I could give him this, he left me and moved to his new apartment with his parents.

Dear Hyun-Binaaa,

I Love you so much. You have given me everything that, I want. I really can't believe it, to thought that you're rude. Do you really know how much I love you? Believe it. In all my life I didn't adore someone as I adore you. You're with me when my parents are busy with their work. I spent more time with you and your family than mine. In all my life, I never thought I would be this much happy. I am your one and only. Wish we will have a more memorable and happy life together. To the moon and back, I adore you.

— Bong-Cha

A tear lands on the paper. Shit, why am I crying? I wipe away the tears and pat the letter dry. That's how the letters became smudge. I almost read this letter a thousand times more, and each time I cried. I fold the letter gently and tuck it into my purse.

Every time, I tried to get rid of this love after reading this letter; I fall even hard.

As Taylor said, this was the very first page, not where the storyline ends. My thought will echo your name until I see you again. Until we get together, my thoughts will repeat his name.

Five
Aera

I feel exhausted because of the fight with those foolish punks. They nearly ruined my day. Finally, they both compromised, and now I have a headache. Oh, it hurts a lot. It's dreadful. I enjoy watching fights, but I am sick of this headache. I can handle anything except for this. A shower with bubbles and lavender oil is what I need. I'm hoping it will help alleviate my pain.

I turn on the faucet, and the water is so warm that I want to jump in. Before, let's add soap balls and lavender oil. I adore this type of shower, especially the lavender bath. It's quite refreshing. I jump in, and it feels like heaven to me. I apply the soap generously all over my body, and the bubbles provide a soothing sensation. Lavender is excellent for headaches. I have many products "derived from lavender. I've already shaved, so I'm just enjoying the shower.

I get out of the water after twenty minutes and wrap myself in soft white towel. I followed my usual skincare routine and made my way to my room. Bong-Cha and Dalia had returned from college. Bong-Cha comes to my door. "I'm changing. Please allow me some time," I say. She stopped knocking.

They are sitting in the living room. As I stated, we are renting this two-bedroom apartment. Bong-Cha stays in one room while Dalia and I share the other. Bong-Cha's father pays the highest rent possible because she prefers to have her own room. Though she is afraid of ghosts and spends her nights with us, she needs a separate room.

I dressed up and came out, only to find my friend Dalia sleeping on the couch. "No wonder she's a sleepy crybaby," I say as I pulled my bag out from beneath her. Bong-Cha agrees with me, laughing and nodding. "Are you going somewhere?" she inquires.

"Yeah, I'm having trouble getting over the painting. So, I'm curious about the details."

"Did you find any sources to learn about the story?"

"No, not yet," I say, disappointedly.

"Where are you off to now?"

"Seeing the painting evokes a sensation I have never experienced before. Seeing it brings me comfort, so I'm going back to the museum."

I don't want her to accompany me. I noticed that she seemed down at college today, but I'm not sure why. Maybe she's tired now, so I think she should rest here. I left the house by myself and waited for a cab. It's getting late. I didn't hail a cab. After fifteen minutes, I got one. I get in and tell the driver to take me to the Royal Museum.

Why on earth am I coming here? I have despise this place since I was a child. What am I doing? When I was with my father, I got lost here. As a result, I began to dislike museums. And, also due to my boring history classes, I lost interest in history. But there is something mysterious about this painting; I sense an untold story lurking behind it.

When I start walking towards the art gallery, I feel as someone is following me. I brush it off and moved on. While walking alone, I have a habit of counting my steps. So, I begin to count. One, two, three, four.......

I keep counting all the way to the art gallery. I could hear my footsteps in the silence. I look around, unsure. I am unable to see anyone. Not even a single individual. So, what exactly am I hearing? I am aware of footsteps behind me.

Tap, tap, tap... It eventually rises. I didn't turn back because I am afraid. Strange thoughts have started to occupy my mind. Is someone following me? Will I be kidnapped? Is the kidnapper going to kill me? What if he's a serial killer who dismembers me for his pleasure? You should be brave in this situation, dear brain. Don't think of anything negative that will frighten me. I beg my mind to stop thinking such disturbing thoughts.

Fear fills my mind with negative thoughts. No, I shouldn't feel this way. Think like Bong-Cha, Aera. Think. Come on, you can do it. I console myself and summon courage. I take a deep breath and exhale the oxygen from my lungs. I sit down and pretend to tie my shoelaces. The space between my legs enables me to see what's behind me. I finished my race and I can't believe what I'm seeing now.

With my eyes widened, I rise from the ground in shock. I turn back slowly, and there is no one behind me or in front of me. I'm completely perplex. Where did those sounds come from?

"Hello, is there anyone here?" I inquire cautiously. But I don't get a response, so I assumed it was just my delusions.

My heart is racing as I approach the painting, and I can hear it in my head. I feel terrific. My heart is racing as fast as it can. I'm not sure why my heart is racing. Is this due to the painting? Am I experiencing any health issues? I'm completely perplexed. As my headache intensifies, I decide to leave this place. But I just can't leave without seeing that painting. My entire focus is on that one painting.

Even if I try to leave, I can't. So, I decided to leave after seeing the painting. I approach the painting with each step. Just a few steps left to reach it. Eventually, I go near. I take my last step. I hear them again, those footsteps. But all of a sudden, it stops. Heart beats, racing faster and faster inside my head. I place my right hand on my left chest. My heart beats normally. What the heck is happening to me? Why am I hearing these sounds? It increases as much as possible. "Stop, stop!" I yell desperately.

I stumble. I sit with my knees bent to the ground and my hands covering my ears. It gradually slows down. Though I can sense something in my dark, empty vision, I squeeze my eyes shut as tightly as possible. All

I can see is a heart beating faster. It seems to be the final few beats of it. I see some hues, but they aren't true colours. It's all red, and I see some tears.

Crap, it's terrible, I think as I hear a loud beep inside my head. It appears that I am going insane. Everything I saw in my illusion came back to me. I did not leave out any elements. I just remembered the entire vision I had.

I should check on my health. It feels as though something is sucking my brain inside my head. Why am I experiencing such unusual pain? I was fine, not great, a week ago, I was excessively good. And then I find myself exhaust and sick for no apparent reason. Something, I'm not sure what it is. But I feel like a complete mess inside. I'm not the same person I used to be.

I approach the painting with all of these confusions in my mind. When I see the portrait, a mix of peace and pain washes over me. "Why? Why am I talking to you? I don't know what I'm doing here. I am not the kind of person who looks for a painting's history. Logically, I don't even know what I am supposed to do with you. Look at me now. I am talking to a painting. Does it make sense?"

I know I don't get anything because I'm talking to a painting. It is unable to respond in any way. Oh my God, what should I do? Should I stop dwelling on this painting and move forward with my life? Or... I groan and pat the back of my head. I take a step forward. I want to see the painting one more time, so I turn around and take a look. My gaze is suddenly captivated by the girl's eyes in this painting. My entire attention is focused on those eyes. They appear to intend to say something to me. Something I am unaware of.

I have a quick thought: should I stop working on this portrait, or should I keep going? I rarely make decisions on my own, but I made one on the spur of the moment. I can't get those eyes out of my head. I can feel the pain, love, and desire to live. I can see every emotion that the artist depicted in this portrait.

I glance at my watch and realize that I have been studying this enigmatic artwork for over an hour. I should leave right away, or Bong-Cha will reprimand me. It makes sense that she would come here to check me out.

I spot seeing a boy as I am heading towards the exit. He appears to be five; he could be four or six. I'm not sure. The young boy and his mother are six feet away from where I stand. Not less than ten times, his mother has warned him not to touch anything. He appears exhaust and nags her to take him home, but she says nothing.

Since I often carry candies with me, I examine my bag. So, I take a few and hand them to the young boy. His pupils widen, and I could see joy there. It's somewhat soothing. He is working on the sweets when I ask him for his name. So, I left him with a goodbye. He says goodbye with a hand gesture. He waves his hands until I disappear from his view.

Six
Aera

I abruptly awaken and look for my phone to check the time. It's 8:05 a.m., and then I sit on the couch and discover I have received many texts. I am surprised by who is texting me because, naturally, I don't receive many text messages. Except from my best friends, I usually receive calls from my parents.

I open the phone and discover that it's from my mother.

Hello, Aera. How are things going for you?

Your father and I had planned to see you this week, but he is unable to do so. So, I'll be there tomorrow, excited to meet you and your friends. Love you.

What the hell is happening? Why is she coming today? I dislike being around my mother. That doesn't mean I despise my mother. She is more outspoken and emotional. Yes, I need her love, but she sometimes overwhelms me. I'm concerned about my friends. I'm not sure how they feel. Maybe they don't enjoy having my mother around. First, I need to tell them.

Later, I notice that Dalia isn't here. She usually sleeps until 11:00, which surprises me. "Where did she gone?"

I rush into the other room to inform Bong-Cha about my mother. They aren't there when I open the door. Did they abandon me and go somewhere else? I'm furious. I've gone to make coffee. On my way to the kitchen, I hear laughter and catch a whiff of something delicious.

Dalia and Bong-cha are both unable to cook. They always try to cook but end up causing chaos in the kitchen. Either, I don't know how to cook. Where is the smell coming from?

"Hey, Aera, you're finally up," Bong-Cha exclaims. "Take a look at who's standing here," she continues.

I see my mom standing in the kitchen. I finally hugged my mother. I miss her hugs and her delicious food. "Momma, what are you cooking? It smells fantastic."

"Hobakjuk, gimbap," she mentioned.

Hobakjuk is a type of pumpkin porridge, which tastes and smells delicious. One of my favourite foods is Gimbap. It is prevalent in Korea. Ham, egg, vegetables, pickled radish, and rice are all rolled up in a dried seaweed sheet.

"Oh, Mom, I'm starving."

"No, freshen up and have some coffee first," she urges lovingly.

This irritates me the most. She always tells me what to do, which I sometimes accept but not always.

I noticed Bong-Cha raising our small, foldable dinner table. We haven't used it since the day we got it. It's simply sleeping in the room. Dalia walks past me as I enter my room to take a shower. "Have you showered?" I asked curiously.

"Yes, right now, and I'm going to have breakfast."

"Wait? You're such a slacker that you don't get up this early, and what about taking a shower? You rarely do this, don't you?"

"It's because of the food. I dislike making the meal wait for me. And you better hurry or I'll have yours too," she chuckled as she dashed to the dining room.

"Touch it and you're fucking dead," I yell, and my mom responds, "watch your language, Aera.'

When I return to the dining area after the shower, Bong-Cha asks me to bring her phone. So, I entered her room. I rarely come here. This room is more amazing than ours, filled with books and decorative items. It has a vintage feel to it. Bong-Cha prefers letters over phone calls and text messages. She writes to her father regularly. She also keeps a diary. Bong-Cha is flawless in every way. I sometimes envy her perfection.

I look all over her room, but her phone is nowhere to be found. Nowhere.

"Bong-Cha, where is your phone?" I inquire.

"It's not here. I looked around the room," I add.

"And what about the drawer?" she asks.

Then I open the table drawer, and there it is, the phone. But I am drawing my attention to something. It's a letter, and I'm intrigued by it. So, I chose to read it. But something inside me told me no. I felt it was weird, so I left.

My interest is piqued when I return. At the very least, I should check the recipient at least. Whom did she address the letter to? I return to the drawer and lift the letter, skimming through its entire contents. It's a love letter.

"I guess_____

No, not a guess. Definitely, it is!" I mumble.

Then I noticed the name she had written in the bottom right corner. They fill my eyes with regret, and tears are streaming down my cheeks. I slam the door shut behind me. Why did she write him a letter? This is unbearable for me. An unfamiliar ache swells within me, obstructing my throat, and I am unable to speak.

The only thing that came to mind is the name. The name written in the letter. It's beyond my comprehension. My mind keeps repeating the name "Hyun Bin" that I saw.

"Did you get the phone, Aera?" Bong-Cha asks.

"Coming," I say.

I handed her the phone. She takes my hands in hers and motions for me to sit. But I sit next to Dalia. I'm sure she'll be disappointed. But that irritates me. I am the one who first loved him, and now she is interfering.

Bong-Cha stares at me, and I can see her disappointment. Her gaze caught mine, and I avoided making eye contact.

"So, what's the plan?" Dalia inquire. I remain mute.

"Guys, I'm asking you," she continues.

"I'm not sure, how about the park?" says Bong-Cha.

"Perfect," I say.

I don't want to be rude. She is the one I care about the most. Hyun-Bin is just my crush. Even though it hurts to see my friend secretly loving my crush.

Dalia invites my mother to join us. She thought it would be entertaining if she come along. My friends are starting to like her. That is too good.

We headed to the park near our house. This park is where we usually spend our weekends. Perfect for jogging and for elderly individuals to pass their time.

"Look who's here?" Dalia exclaims. I turn to see the yang pair. I tell my mother about them. They greet my mum with a bow. I don't think my mother would be that accepting of LGBTQ+ people, but she is polite and respectful towards them. She even deliver some life advices.

"What exactly are you doing here?" I am curious.

"Vibing," Hyun-Yang chuckle.

"Stop joking. We're here with Hyun-Bin for a walk," says Yang-Min.

When I hear his name, my heart trembles. My hands are trembling, and I can feel the emptiness within. I used to feel warmth from him, but now I'm afraid to confront him.

"God_____ I shouldn't have come here," I mumble under my breath.

He eventually arrived after spotting us. I'm drawn to his dark eyes every time I see them. He's dressed in a grey hoodie and black trousers. There's nothing sexier than his hands and the veins that run through them. It looks even better with his sleeves rolled up.

He is facing me and standing near my mother. He smiled at me before turning to chat with my mother. My mom seems happy when she talks to him.

I've recently noticed him eyeing Bong-Cha; he frequently does that when talking to my mother. At last, he said "Howdy" to her, followed by "Oh, good," she says shyly.

My eyes becomes hot and teary. It brings me joy to see them together. I am happy for them, but I love him with all my heart, and it hurts to see him with someone else. I wipe my eyes with my sleeves and pretend that everything is fine. No one notices the sadness in my eyes, not even my mother, but Bong-Cha did.

She grabs my hands away from them and pulls me a few steps away. She knows how to make me feel better. She extended a full hug like she always does. She softly pats my shoulder, and it feels warm. In a single hug, all my regrets vanished.

"Are you okay?" she questions as she lifts my face.

"Yeah, fine," I lie.

"I know you're upset since this morning, and now something else has made you sad. I can sense Aera, I can sense everything, everything that hurts you," she says, looking into my eyes.

"Yeah, Don't worry. I'm fine now." I lie once more.

"I can tell whether you're okay or not. Don't be sad. If you don't want to tell me right now. Please let me know when you feel comfortable. Okay?" she says, grabbing my hands.

I hug her again and smile as I whisper "Okay, donkey" into her ear.

She turns to face me, taps my nose, and says, "Okay, donkey."

Seven
Aera

It's strange to be here. Facing my loved one while he is standing with his crush, it intensifies the pain. So, I moved away and sat on a bench next to a large tree. The atmosphere is pleasant, and witnessing children playing brings me joy.

I noticed two children playing under the tree. A boy and a girl. The girl appears to be more mature than the boy. She instructs him to complete any tasks necessary while playing. This demonstrates her dominance. How adorable, I remarked. I spent a few minutes watching them before noticing a man standing a few meters away and staring at me. Initially, I assumed he was watching the kids, but recently, I realized he was watching me. He's keeping an eye on me.

It's strange. I've never met him. Who is he? I doubt myself. He appears to be in his forties, with wrinkles on both sides of his eyes. He is wearing a jacket over a brown high-neck t-shirt and pants. He gives me a friendly smile. A little grin. It's adorable how his eyes crinkle when he smiles. Even though I had never seen him before in our place of residence.

He seems strange, and why is he smiling at me? I kept an eye on him as he approached. He gradually gets closer to me. By looking into his eyes, I can tell he has bad intentions. Those eyes seem lonely, and it is difficult. I feel awkward whenever he looks at me. So, I return to my friends and tightly hold Bong-Cha's hand.

"What happened?" she asked curiously.

I raise my hands and point at him. He smirks again as I lower my hands. "Do you know him?" I questioned, looking at Bong-Cha.

"Who?" she asks sceptically.

"Look over there, him," I say once more.

"Nobody's there, Aera. Look around," she says.

I look back, and he isn't there. My pupils dilate. How could he have vanished in a matter of seconds? I'm completely taken aback.

What is happening to me? I have been sick since this morning. My mother noticed me. And she asks why I appear to be in a bad mood. I tried to explain the situation, but Bong-Cha defended me and handled my mother.

"Nothing, Aunt. She hasn't been feeling well recently. She is becoming increasingly dizzy."

"Aera, are you okay? Are you sick?" my mom asks.

"No, no, Auntie. She's fine. It's just because of stress," Bong-Cha manages again.

Hyun-Bin invites us to join him for coffee. Bong-cha and I both denied it. However, my mother accepted the offer and forced us to come. My mother joins Hyun-Bin, Dalia joins the Yangs, and Bong-cha and I follow. She caresses me by holding my hands tightly. I shouldn't be so hard on her in the morning. I am unhappy with myself.

Then I realize she composed the letter for him in a confessional tone, suggests that she isn't yet his girlfriend. Hyun-Bin approached her in a bashful and hesitant manner. They are not dating. They never confessed their feelings to each other. Maybe they don't realize it, but they have feelings for each other.

I wish I could help them figure things out. I feel silly. This morning, I thought Bong-Cha snached him away from me, and now I'm considering helping them. Literally, I am dumb as hell. I smirk and turn to face Bong-Cha. She returns his smile and asks, "What?" with her eyes. I say "Nothing" with a wink.

We walk for approximately 10 minutes to reach the café because it is a bit far away. I walked away from Bong-Cha and went to see my mother. Hyun-Bin heads back and allows us some privacy. How sweet is he? He took on the position I had left vacant. Yes, he starts walking with Bong-Cha. She clasped her hands across her chest as he approached. Perhaps she is shy. I smirk and begin conversing with my mother. Since my mother arrived, I have not inquired about my father.

"How's Dad?"

"He's doing well, yeah. Actually, it was his intention to pay a surprise visit, but he was occupied with work. That's why he couldn't come," she explains.

"That's okay. He works so hard for us, Mom. I believe he needs rest. Just one more year, Mom, and after my studies, I'll take care of everything," I reassure her, gently rubbing her hands.

"You sound more mature than you did before," she says. I can see the emotions in her eyes.

"My daughter is growing faster," she adds, smiling.

"Finally, we're here." Dalia says. We head inside and placed our orders. The artwork, wall hangings, and overall atmosphere of the cafe are stunning.

"This place is incredible," I say, to which everyone agrees.

"I believe Bong-Cha prefers this location," I continue, but she just stares at me blankly.

"Why?" Hyun-Bin inquires.

"Because she's a philocalist," I reply.

"Means?" he inquires.

"Lover of beauty," Bong-Cha says, and I chuckle.

"Oh, I see. But who on earth taught you that phrase? This is the first time I've heard this," he begins.

"Bong-Cha," I reply.

"She loves such things," I add.

Bong-Cha and I proceed to take our orders. We all ordered iced Americanos. Bong-Cha lifts the rest while I lift a couple. She inquired as I begin to take my first steps forward.

'When did you find out?"

I refuse to tell the truth about the letter I read.

"When I saw the way he looked at you," I replied.

We return, and I let her seat next to him. So, they can construct anything between themselves. Oh, God, she is very shy, and he is also quite shy. Nothing will happen if they remain silent. We had good time drinking and talking. It's a happy morning. It must be the nicest morning ever.

"Hey Dalia," Yang-Min starts.

"We're going to play video games. Would you like to come along?" She accepted their offer and joined them. They're on their way to their apartment. The Yang couple has been living together since the first semester.

Bong-Cha is on her way to the library to research the history of Silla. So, Hyun-Bin proposed to accompany her. That's a good move to get closer. So, my mother and I should return to the house to cook lunch.

After they left, my mother and I went outside, and observe someone staring at us for a long time. As I have stated, my mother is very sociable and she approached him. I took her hands in mine and asked, "Where are you going?"

"I noticed this man staring at us for a long time. So, I'm going to ask why," she starts.

I recognize him and realize that he is the same person who had glanced and smiled at me earlier in the park.

I'm confident that he's the one. I come to a halt in front of my mother and state, "He has been stalking me since the morning, Mom. It's probably not safe to interact with him."

"Are you sure he's stalking you?" she asked curiously.

"No, but he seems that way," I say.

"No, Aera, I can discern someone's intention just by looking at them, and he didn't seem like a stalker. What if you resemble his daughter or someone else? There would be other causes as well. Let's just talk to him," she sounds foolish.

"But, mom, mom____," I try to stop her but grabs my hands and drags me over to him. She introduced herself and engaged in conversation. He's not as horrible as I imagined. He is completely normal, and he states that he only wants to talk to me.

"Strange," I begin,

"Why would you want to talk to me?" He responds I resemble someone he has already met. I bowed and bid him farewell. Then my mother and I went to the market to buy some vegetables.

We return to our room, and mom requests me to help with the lunch. The day went really well, mainly because of the old man who was incredibly humble and kind. That's not how I should think of him. It is quite dangerous to pass judgment on someone you barely know.

Eight
Bong-Cha

"Do you remember me?" he inquired. My pupils dilate; what he is asking now seems surreal. I try to speak, but my words are clogged, and I couldn't even spit them out. A million thoughts races through my mind.

Did he remember me? Did he still adore me as much as he did when we were kids? A million and one thoughts of love gush. But, like an idiot, my face stays blank. My emotions are overwhelming, but I can't articulate them because I have a blockage in my throat. I try harder and eventually, "What?"

Shit, I am supposed to say 'yes'.

"Nothing, just____

Nothing" he manage and changed the topic.

What should I do now? Instead of 'what', I should have said 'yes'. What if he believes I forgot about him? It will only get worse.

I enjoy spending time with him, but what if I ruin his mood? I should be more mindful and considerate of him.

We complete the entry, and I went to the history section to look for something relevant to the portrait we saw in the museum. I continue my hunt for the book on the shelf. I don't find anything that is similar to what I am looking for.

I'm not sure if I should keep looking, and, I notice an ancient book. It seems too old to be of any use to us. So, I raise my hands and stand on tiptoe to grab the book. However, it is higher than I anticipated.

I lost my footing and fell, landing again on Hyun-Bin. And I realize he followed me all over the library and stood back. I fell on him. I turn to face him.

I just looked him into the eyes. And he did the same thing. My hands are on his chest. It is hot and sexy. Our bodies made contact. I lean back and rest my head on his chest. He ran his fingertips down my spine and wrapped his arms around me.

I take a moment to move closer to him. Very close, as I keep picturing this event in my head. Suddenly, he kissed me. He soak them. His breath smells a tough minty and burnt.

He inserted his tongue and waited for me to enjoy it. I hesitate to respond to him. He senses my hesitation and tightens his grip on my hip as I move forward, but eventually I refuse to kiss him back. He left his grip around me and face me with guilt.

"Hey, here," says the maintenance worker. Thankfully, our librarian did not notice us.

I attempt to stand up. He lifted me, took the book, and rubbed my head. We walk over to a desk and seat. He request me to wait a second before proceeding to the

English part. And he came back with a book. A book with fresh vocabulary and phrases.

"Why this book?" I inquired.

"I'm going to learn more new phrases like the one Aera said this morning," he starts.

He's trying to impress me. That's cute. I love it. He didn't changed at all. He's as lovely as he was in childhood. I can remember, he threw his favourite chocolate for impressing me, because I don't like chocolate.

Sometimes he bought chocolates for me, even though I didn't like them. I ate them for his joy.

I skip through a lot of this book. There is no explanation for the painting's backstory. We only have a limited understanding of the Great Silla's infrastructure and culture.

This book demonstrates that the people of Silla were hard workers, with the female population of Silla being more concerned with beauty and cleanliness. Traditional Korea regarded gold as a source of pride, and the emperors' crowns and thrones were fashioned of pure gold.

I return to replace this book and run across this man again. The person I met earlier in the museum. Yes, we have a new librarian.

"What are you looking for?" he asks.

"Silla's history," I say.

"I know a little about Silla; I can help you, but not right now. I'm a bit busy. How about evening?" he says.

"Sure thing, I'll be here at 4:00 p.m.," I say, returning back to Hyun-Bin.

I notice him memorizing phrases like a child. I could spend the entire day simply gazing at him while he reads. When he reads, he appears sexier. I admire males who read. It's scorching hot when it comes to Hyun-Bin.

He turns and glances around for me. It drew his gaze to mine. I hide behind a bookshelf. He looks for me again and stands up from his seat to search for me. So, I approached him by myself and tapped him on the back.

"Where you gone? I'm worried" he says.

"Nothing, just met the librarian and he said he'll help me with figuring out things. So, I was just talking with him before," I replied.

He avoids making eye contact with me. Perhaps it's because of that kiss. It should not have happened before. We simply got a little too close and are now back in our awkward state.

After a few moments, he received a phone call from his grandmother. I'm familiar with her, and Hyun-Bin has always been her world. He used to spend his evenings with his grandmother, and he constantly remains with her when his parents are at work.

After the conversation, he begins talking about her grandmother, saying that he had been living with his grandmother since the day his mother died, and that his father had married other women and resided in Seoul. He now lives alone in his own apartment and visits his grandmother once a month.

I'm unfamiliar with any of these. He had experienced far more challenges than I could ever imagine. I'm concerned about him. I wish I could have been there for him, sharing his sorrows and pains, and taking care of him. All of these thoughts have been running through my mind.

I'm on my way to our apartment after spending time with Hyun-Bin. Aera and her mother would be waiting for me at approximately twelve thirty. I took off as quickly as I could.

On my walk home, I replay the scene in my mind repeatedly. It feels like a nightmare. I believe he feels remorseful for kissing me without my consent. Perhaps he is re-enacting the same scene in an embarrassing manner.

My mother once told me that she and my father were close friends. She recounted a story of a night when they went for a walk while it was snowing outside. My father stumbled and accidentally kissed my mother.

My father began ignoring her out of humiliation from that day forward. He continued to ignore her until my mother confessed her feelings to him.

What if Hyun-Bin does the same thing? What if he ignores me because he is embarrassed? Oh my God, that would aggravate our relationship. As soon as I get home, I should text him.

Dalia is sweeping the kitchen when I arrive. I have a spare key to our apartment, so I entered and found her in a terrible condition. Aunt is directing her to clean properly, and she is irritated because she doesn't even do it herself.

Aunt forces her to complete the assignment flawlessly after a long fight. I am sitting on the couch, laughing uncontrollably at her. It is truly hilarious to see her perform such things.

"Stop laughing," she yells.

"Sorry, but I can't help," I burst out with laughter.

"I have to take a shower again," she spat out frustrated.

"You should," I say with giggles.

She dashed inside their room, gathered her belongings for a shower, and shut the bathroom door. Aunt asked me to help her set the dining table.

So, I set up the dining table, and Aunt approaches with all the food she had prepared. I pick up a few items, while she handles the chopsticks, bowls, and other dishes. We set up a grill for barbecuing pork. Aera and I both enjoy grilled ribs.

I didn't notice Aera because she wasn't there. "Where is Aera?" I inquire of Aunt.

"I asked her to get us some drinks. Soju with grilled pork ribs would be nice," she explains.

"Yeah, that's true, Auntie," I agree.

She lit the barbecue, and I tossed some pork ribs on it. I spray it with oil and flip it over to ensure thorough cooking. The marinated pork ribs had been thoroughly soaked in salt and oil, allowing the spices to penetrate the meat. The aroma while grilling it is amazing. I'm tempted to eat because I can hear it grilling. I can feel my nose and tongue tingling.

Dalia finishes her shower when Aera returns with soju. We all sit down around the table and begin to taste the meal. When the flavour of the meat spreads across my taste buds, it's just as incredible as I imagined.

Nine
Aera

Visiting the museum and viewing the masterpiece has recently become a habit of mine. I couldn't get this obsession out of my mind. I'm not sure, but I think I like it.

My friends and I typically take this route to the bus stop. While strolling, we talk and tease each other. But now that I am alone, I can truly appreciate the beauty of this place and the route I am taking.

Cherry trees surrounded on all sides. A nice breeze. I can even hear the wind blowing through. The clouds and sunset. I've admired sunsets since I was a child. When I witness the sunset, I get the impression that it is meant for me. Something I can't even describe.

I take in all these as I walk to the museum. I entered the museum and went to the art section. My steps are becoming larger, and I am getting too close to the artwork. When I arrived, there was a man standing in front of it. I'm intrigued by him. By muttering under my breath, I approach. Who is he?

He is the man I met in the park earlier. What a coincidence that we keep running into each other! He abruptly turned around and said, "Hello, miss! What a shock!"

"Yeah, I'm surprised as well," I say quietly.

"We're destined to meet again and again," he chuckles.

"So, what exactly are you doing here?" he asks.

"I'm just here for a visit; I've recently became obsessed with this painting and want to learn more about it," I explain.

"Are you into art? Or just this one?" He inquired.

"No, I'm not a histrophile; I just became interested in this one because it seems to have an untold backstory. Don't you agree?"

"Yeah, it has," he says.

His conversations are unusual. Too many questions arise within me every time he speaks. And now, what's the deal with this answer? Yeah, it has.

I controlled my tongue and asked, "What do you mean?"

"Every art has its own backstory, Aera," he begins.

"Tell me, what do you feel when you look at this painting?" he inquired.

"Nothing special. Love, a tragic emotion that remains unknown to the world. The girl's eyes reveal unfathomable anguish and anticipation. That's all I can feel," I say.

"You're perfect," he says, glancing at the image.

I like the way he speaks; it's humble and kind. We talk a lot about this painting, and he mentions that the boy in the picture appears filled with unfathomable remorse and guilt. I like the way he explains it.

We set out together, and he walks with me the entire way. I'm hungry, starving. It's almost seven o'clock. I had eaten nothing since the afternoon.

My stomach made an 'Er____' sound, and the man laughs at me. "Are you hungry?" he later inquired. In humiliation, I lower my head and gaze at my feet.

He repeats. "Miss, are you hungry?"

"Yeah, terribly," I mumble.

"There's a corn dog stand on the way to your house," he rubs my head. "You're only a few steps away from the location. Go there and get some."

"You're coming, right? Aren't you?" I ask.

"No, I have some work to do. You'd better get home safely," he says, turning to walk in the opposite direction. I shout with joy, "See you tomorrow," as he walks away.

I can see people on my way, once after I start walking the road is grows dark. However, walking alone at night can be unsettling. I take small steps forward until I come across a corn dog stand. It is on the left side of the road.

"Excuse me," I say to the shopkeeper. She is preoccupied with serving others. That stall is so small that it doesn't even qualify as a stall. They placed a stall in a mobile van. The truck is parked, and chairs are arranged in the sides for customers to sit.

The lady finally approaches. I placed an order for five corn dogs. I told her to pack four and serve one to me. She returns with my order, and I paid 5000 won.

On the way; I eat a corn dog topped with ketchup and mustard, which is fantastic. I want to thank the man for accompanying me on my way, as well as for the corn dog.

Finally, I arrive at our flat. Something doesn't feel right, and it's quiet here. If my friends are here, it won't be this quiet. What happened to them? Are they sleeping or have they gone somewhere else? I doubt.

Then I went through the bag looking for the keys, shit_____ I forgot, I gave it to my mother this morning. I should go ring the doorbell right now. I press the bell, and Bong-Cha approaches to open the door in a matter of seconds.

They don't do these. They always make me wait for what feels like an eternity. Today has taken me by surprise. Suddenly, miracles are happening. Ha-ha_____ when the door swings open, and I take my first step inside, Bong-Cha hugs me and says, "Dalia got stuck with your mom's gossip. I'd gotten away, but she is a pity. Help us."

She let me go, and I went to see what was going on. Dalia is literally in a deplorable state. She'd go insane if I approach a little late. I move on after dropping the corn dogs on the couch.

"Mom, what's going on?"

Dalia rushes behind me after hearing my voice, Bong-Cha is laughing hysterically, and my mother is perplexed. She doesn't even know what I'm talking about.

"Everything is in order. I was just telling Dalia about our neighbours and their stories, Aera. It was a lot of fun; you can ask Dalia about it," she adds innocently.

"We're not aunties, Bong-Cha, and Dalia doesn't like such gossips. If I'm a few minutes later, she'd go insane," I yell, but not harshly.

I see disappointment in my mother's eyes, but I couldn't help her. I'd like to inform my mother that I dislike these.

My mother is not narrow-minded; she understands me. So, there's nothing I can say to explain her. She will be well tomorrow.

However, this b*tch Dalia noticed my mother's dejected expression and rushed to her side, saying, "No Aera, I am fine. You shouldn't yell at your mom like that. Dare you repeat this," she admitted as she hugged my mother.

What's going on? For God's sake I am speaking on her behalf, and she made the same side goal. She's irritating me.

There's nothing I can do about it now; she's been stuck again, and I will not aid her any longer. I walk over to the couch, grab the bag of corn dogs, wave it in the air, and ask, "Who wants corn dogs?"

"Me," all three says at the same time. They also take their fair share. They did not know that I already had one. I remove the silver wrapper and begin eating another corn dog.

Ten
Bong-Cha

Aera agrees to join me after her mother slept with Dalia. We rarely sleep together. I usually sleep alone in my room, but if I wake up around midnight, I go to my friend's room and sleep with them. Because of my mother's bedtime stories, I am a little afraid of ghosts.

Aera is a light sleeper who is prone to being startled. So, I gave her my earmuffs. She lies next to me and falls asleep within five to ten minutes. I watch her sleep for a while.

I'm not tired; I'm an owl. I'm frequently awake until almost one o'clock, either drawing or reading a book. Reading literature has become an extension of myself. My days only feel productive if I read at least one page. I began reading at seven and am now twenty, almost thirteen years bong.

I started reading books in the fantasy genre and have recently transitioned to reading hot romance and romantic comedies. I imagine myself with a boyfriend like Aron Warner, who considers Julie to be his entire universe.

I wish to be in someone else's world. I want them to be centred on me. They should not be able to see anything beyond me. Someone should be thinking about me for almost twenty hours a day. And the individual should only be Hyun-Bin. I only want his undivided attention, love, care, and kisses. While thinking about kissing, I notice my cheeks turning crimson. I remember that morning.

Ah, shit.

I completely forgot to text him. What should I do now? Should I contact him? I take out my phone to text him.

Me: Hey, are you awake?

I want to talk. Can you call?

Before pressing the send button, I delete it. I deleted everything and text once more,

Me: Hey!

I want to talk about that morning. Shall we?

No, no, no, I deleted it once more. I feel empty and uninteresting. I want to say something lovely.

Me: Hey, Hyun-Bin.

Me: I want to talk about something. Are you free tomorrow?

Me: Let's meet at sugar café at five P.M

This sounds friendly and perfect. I hit the send button and wait for his response. I have been waiting for over 30 minutes and still haven't received a response. Perhaps he's napping. How does he appear when he is sleeping? I suppose it'll be sweet to watch him sleep.

I visit his profile on Instagram. We're not following each other, but I can see his posts because his profile is public. I'm practically stalking him on social media. He's having about 7k followers, but I only have 376. His profile appears to be that of a celebrity. And on mine, I only post artwork and books. We have around forty mutual, yet he hasn't made any follow requests, and he's even following Aera.

I noticed he liked Aera's posts. Aera is a lovely young lady, an active cat, and a talker. Most of our college lads have crush on her, but she have shown no interest. I secretly envy her fame. I'm curious, who is her crush, and does she secretly admire anyone?

When I'm thinking about her, I observe Aera sleep-talking. It's adorable to see her speaking while she's asleep. I went in close to listen to her because it isn't audible. When I get closer, she is waving her hands in the air and saying, "No, it shouldn't have happened"

What should not have happened? I am curious, and she is talking about Hyun-Bin, that she likes him. She did it again and again.

My heart trembles, and it has broken into pieces. I'm riddled with questions and overwhelmed by guilt.

Am I loving my friend's crush? It's difficult for her to watch him with me; she should have told me sooner. Crap, crap, I made a major error. I should keep my distance from him. I can't share him with anyone else. At the same time, I can't hurt Aera too.

I shouldn't go there the next day. I should cancel the text before he sees it. I remove my phone from the charger and unlock it to unsend the message, but there is a 'seen' mark beneath it. I have no idea what's going to happen.

But he kissed me at the library, and I know it's not an accidental kiss. Which implies that he is interested in me; what about Aera? What should I say to her? How can I accept love that causes harm to my friend? Oh God!

When I awake the next morning, the first thing I notice is Aera's face. Last night, I was thinking about this situation and fell asleep near the bed. She finally opens her eyes and says, "Gummorning" in a husky voice.

"Morning" I reply.

I checked my phone and I got three notifications from Hyun-Bin. I unlock and read them.

Hyun Bin: I would be glad to,

Hyun Bin: Actually, I was thinking about yesterday, but felt a little hesitant.

Hyun Bin: I'll be there on time ♥

I made a complete mess; how am I going to deal with this situation? I'm terrified of losing both my lover and a friend at the same time. I went to take a shower, still perplexed.

I undress and turn on the shower, standing under the water and crying louder, too loudly.

I check myself in the bathroom mirror after taking a shower. My eyes became very red. I examine myself carefully, tucking my wet hair behind my ears. I'm not that good; I have small eyes with mono lids, a light skin colour that isn't as fair as Aera's, medium height, and very unattractive bodily traits. When it comes to my appearance, I sometimes have an inferiority complex. Even if I despise myself, this girl Aera admires me and admires every action I take in whatever situation. How am I going to offend her?

This question persists in my mind. I don't want to be in a bad mood in front of my pals; what if I yell at them? That would worsen the situation. As a result, I skip breakfast. I grabbed my diary, pen, and backpack before leaving the house.

I'm at a loss about where to go; I'm a coffee junkie, and I can't start my day without at least a sip of coffee. So, I went to a coffee shop near our residence. When I'm feeling down, I usually go to that place.

I went there and ordered a coffee latte. I take out my diary and jot down everything that happened the day before yesterday. I write one by one in order, and when I get to the kiss, I realized I am weeping. My tears stream down onto the table in front of my notebook.

As I am wiping them away, the server arrives and delivers my Latte and two sugar packs near me. I usually add more sugar to my coffee, but today I want to taste the bitterness of the coffee, so I'm skipping the sugar. When I notice her, the server glances at me briefly before averting her gaze.

"Are you okay?" she questioned later.

"Yeah, I'm fine," I lie.

"Are you sure? You appear upset, dear," she adds.

"I'm fine_____," I try to repeat, but I burst out crying. I have a wonderful friendship with this woman here, and it's early in the morning, so there are no customers around.

She gives a gentle hug and inquires, "What happened Bong Bong?"

She is the only person who refers to me as bong bong. I forced a bitter smile and said everything, everything that happened yesterday made me sad. She remains eerily silent for a long time. When I finish recounting my entire story to her, she simply states, "Life is comprised of moments, whether they are positive or negative, and these moments are the building blocks that make life intriguing."

"Do whatever feels right for you," she adds.

By stating this, she returns to take an order from a customer who approaches. She is the reason I come here more often. She always makes me feel better when I'm feeling down.

I paid for my coffee, smile at her, and she smiles back. As I exit the café, I make a decision about what to do next. I'm no longer perplexed; I'm not going to meet him today. I am a firm believer in fate.

He will always find his way back to me if he is meant to be mine.

Eleven
Aera

I look everywhere for her; where has she gone? I had seen her an hour before. And why didn't she have breakfast? She rarely does anything like this. She's been acting strange since I asked her about Hyun-Bin. Am I doing anything wrong? She is almost certainly at the library; I should go get some food and meet her there. She cannot suppress her hunger.

I hurriedly finished my meal and then rushed to my room to grab my belongings, especially my phone. At that point, my mother called to inquire about the market route. I asked her to stay at home and promised to get vegetables when I returned.

She ended up giving me a paper roll filled with the grocery list. "Do we really need all of these?" I scream.

"Do as I say," she abruptly interrupts the conversation and marches to the kitchen with the precision of a soldier.

"God, she really creeps the shit out of me," I mutter as I walk away.

The cherry blossom season is almost here, and I can already see a few flowers blooming. My birthday is almost here. I'm going to be twenty-one in three weeks. My father often tells me that I have a special affinity for cherry blossoms, but I'm not quite sure why.

My phone starts ringing, so I answer it, and it's Bong-Cha calling. I quickly press the answer button.

"Hello," she said.

"Hey," I say, feeling clueless.

"Actually, I had some business to attend to, so I left without having breakfast. I'm sorry," she says quietly.

"All right, that's fine. Where are you now?" I am curious.

"I went to the library, but no one was there. I have no more business out so, I think I should get back home," she says.

"Ask Mom if she needs anything. I'm on my way back home. I can purchase," she adds.

"Yeah, I'll send you a photo," I say, chuckling.

"What? A photograph?" She has no idea.

"Yes, Mum asked me to get a few things and gave me a list. You said you'd buy, didn't you?" I laugh once more.

"Area_____," she murmured, her voice low and nasty. I will email her the grocery list before she refuses. Thank God, she saved me from having to go to the market and bargain. I'm not that kind of person.

I have no reason to be here. What should I do now? I raise my head and gaze up at the sky. I can feel the sunlight on my eyes. It's warm, and I like it. The sunlight abruptly disappears. I open my eyes, and I see two eyes staring back at me. I return my gaze for a few seconds; all I can see are those cold, profound feelings that have yet to be articulated. I close my eyes and experience vivid visuals in my mind, accompanied by a loud beeping sound in my ears. I collapse; my ears ring.

People are staring at me; some are trying to help me, and one man lifts me and seats me on a bench in a café. They approached me and offered me water before calling an ambulance. I requested not to call an ambulance. So, they moved.

What will happen to me? Should I consult a doctor? I'm not sure.

Ah, it freaks me out.

Slowly, I decided to return to our flat, I couldn't help but wonder how my mother would react if she saw me in this state. She'll be concerned. I took a step back and went to the park where I used to go often with my friends. Children are one's only source of joy and comfort. As if I am my father's.

I wish I could return to those idyllic childhood days when I had a friend. We used to play in the shade of a tree. He used to refer to himself as the son of a warrior. My parents discovered that he was my imaginary friend when I was eight. As a result, they showered me with attention. Days passed, and I lost him, but he lives on in my memories.

"May I please sit here?" a friendly voice approaches.

"Sure," I say without looking at the guy.

"Why are you alone? Where have your friends gone?" he asks.

I raise my head and see him, the man I had met before. He is standing near where I am seated on the bench. I wake up and bow, then offer him my seat, which we shared.

"My friends are preoccupied with jobs. So, I came here for some fresh air," I explained.

"Why do you look so sad?" he inquired.

When I hear him ask this, my pupils dilate. I mean, how did he know that? "No, I'm fine," I reply, remaining silent.

"You're not fine. Look into my eyes and tell me you're fine," he says as he turns to face me.

What's the big deal about looking into his eyes? I turn around and try to look at him, but I can't help myself from crying and I can't stop.

He wraps his arms around me and rubs my shoulder, saying, "It's okay, Aera, it's okay."

"You shouldn't have to pretend you're fine when you're experiencing genuine pain. It's perfectly fine to cry if you're in pain," his arms still around me, warm and cosy.

"What bothers you? Tell me," he continues.

"Bong-Cha is in love with the person I love; I can't bear it," I sob once again.

"What about that guy? Does he love you or...?" he questions.

"He is completely in love with Bong-Cha. I can tell by the way he looks at her." I sob and wipe my tears.

"Love isn't forced, Aera; it comes naturally. You should have feelings for the person, and those feelings should be mutual."

"I know, I'm not trying to make him love me," I begin.

"Then? Why are you so upset?" he went on to say.

"It isn't hurting as much as I thought, and that's the worst part," I say, followed by a long silence.

"Then it isn't love," he simply states.

What? What would it be if it wasn't love? I liked everything he did. I am perplexed because I admire his every action. "What is it, if it isn't love? Infatuation?" I yell out of frustration.

"Maybe!"

"Love, it's not an easy thing, my girl. It will surprise you and leave you with mixed emotions. Makes you do everything for that person, including sacrificing yourself. That is the definition of love."

"Do you have such feelings for him?" he asks. I remain completely silent and breathless. Every word he utters is powerful. They are working as hard as they can. I didn't feel this way about anyone else. Even not for my parents.

"You, okay?" he asked.

"Yeah, I'm _____"

"I'm completely clear now, and I need to get home." I left without even saying goodbye. I'm in a hurry to get somewhere. I ran as far as I could. I just want to stay out of his way.

Oh, shit!!!!

My cheeks had turned bright red from embarrassment. When I realize his comments and my feelings for Hyun-Bin are merely infatuation, I feel ashamed. But, God, the way this man talked about love. It's fantastic.

Aww, this man is something.

Something magical...

Later, I realized that I was standing in the middle of the road, wondering about what had happened. I should go somewhere, but where? What should I do next? I press my lips together, contemplating where to go. I then decided to go to the museum. It's the ideal place to spend a day, but before I go, I grab my phone and call my classmate Tae-Moon. He's a quiet, polite man.

Time flew by, and it's now six o'clock. Tae-Moon's visit was enjoyable. He's always courteous. He told me more about art and that specific painting, even though he didn't know much about them. He stated that it was just this year that it was put into an exhibit. It may have been previously investigated. Later, after finishing our meal, I informed Mum that I couldn't join her for lunch. She became angry and started yelling, which made me feel overwhelmed and upset.

The clouds appear dark and cold as I make my way back home. It will begin to rain soon. So, I rushed as fast as I could.

It begins with mist, and when it touches my body, it is gentle, mild, and profound. Deep. It is enjoyable for me. So, I kept my phone in my bag to prevent it from getting wet. Then I just stand there, admiring the mist. I raised my head to face the mist, which made my face and lips damp. I stay for a few minutes before realizing it is going to rain hard, so I rush. Just a few blocks from my house.

I came to a halt as someone forcefully touches me on the shoulder, not with the intention of hurting me, but it does cause a little pain. When I turned around, it was Hyun-Bin. What on earth is he doing here?

"What's up?" inquired. He and I are both drenched. He appears frightened and depressed. He takes my hands in his and inquires about Bong-cha. He tells me everything about the meeting, the library, and the kiss___ I'm crying, but it's hard to see through the rain. I am aware that my feelings for him are not romantic. It's simply a matter of attraction.

Then he hands me a note and tells me to deliver it to Bong-Cha. He pleads with me to do this favour for him.

"I won't refuse because it's about my friend, and you're my friend too," I explain as I take the letter from him.

He wrapped it in plastic wrap. What a genius.

"Waterproof, huh?" Waving it in front of him, I smile. Then I hide it inside my bag, and when I start walking, he yells out my name rushes towards me, and hugs me. It's as warm as my mother's and Bong-Cha's. I hug him back and discover what he means to me. He let me go and rubbed my head, saying, "Go home and get dry first, then give this to her. There's no need to press the matter, okay?"

He returns and continues to turn around, watching me until I enter our flat.

Twelve
Bong-Cha

Aera dashes inside as I open the door to see who rang the doorbell. Her clothing is soaked from the rain, and her hair is dishevelled. She looks like a poor, unruly child. Noticing that she is shivering, I offer her a towel. She refused and begins rummaging through her bag for something. I was perplexed, so I took the bag off and tossed it on the couch. Then, I told her to dry her hair. She rushes to the bag once again, pushing me aside, and takes out a piece of paper. A wet piece of paper covered in plastic.

"What's this? Aera," I ask her.

She extended her hand towards me handed me the letter and said, "This is for you. It comes from Hyun-Bin," and inquired about what had occurred between us. I'm speechless. How can I convey to her everything that happened between us? So, I remain silent.

"I am well-versed in everything Bong-Cha; you invited him to hang out today, but you didn't show up. Why are you behaving in this manner? He is a good boy, and most importantly, he is completely your type," she begins.

"I don't love him" I lie.

"You love him, you really do. Stop acting as if everything is fine. You can't stop loving him," she shouts while standing on a doormat near the door. I'm annoyed with her health. I gently took her hands and told her to dry off first, but she refused.

"Tell me, why are you avoiding him, Bong-Cha? You can't unlove him," she repeats once more.

"You can't, either" I yell back out of frustration.

Her eyes begin to cry, and she turns moist, but this time from her tears. She's so close to me that her tears are falling on my feet. She bowed her head and remained silent. And so am I. I did not approach her to discuss anything. I want her to tell me the truth about her feelings for him.

After a couple of minutes, she kills the silence by saying, "Yes, I do. I do love him with all my heart. But__" Again she goes silent.

"But that wasn't true love. I realized it. And love should be mutual, right? I developed feelings for him as a result of how he handles me. He treats me like you do; he treats me like a child like my father does, and today he hugged me, and I realized that the emotion I am having isn't love. I just admire the way he treats me, like a child, exactly as you treat me." She expresses regret, and her head is still lowered, facing her foot.

I've never heard her speak with such maturity. My friend is maturing. Everything she said today came from the bottom of her heart. She simply said what was on her mind. I don't want to see her sobbing. I lift her face, but she still avoids looking; she simply does not want to meet my sight. I drew her into my arms and clutched her tightly. Then I say, "I don't need anything that hurts you"

Her gaze on me, she looks into my eyes and says, "I'll live my whole life out of guilt if you reject him."

I'm ripping out. All of the things she said are still playing in my head. I have just noticed Aera, when she wiped her eyes and murmured, "You should read this," her attention drifting to the note she had given me. What would he have written if it were from him? I'm not sure. She took the towel that I had provided her before entering her room. I stopped her and said, "Your mother is sleeping in your room, and Dalia has gone out. She hasn't returned yet," I added. She went to take a shower in my room, and I offered her my T-shirt and pants. She heads inside, and I turned the heater on. "Get warm," I say as she disappears inside the bathroom.

It's raining outside, so coffee would be ideal, and Aera is drenched, so she should grab something warm. I go to the kitchen, grabbed a cup of noodles that I bought this morning, and prepare two cups of coffee for both of us. Then I sit down at my desk, holding the letter in my hands. It's raining outside, but the paper just got a little damp and it appears aged. It is completely readable. I opened it and begin reading.

Dear Bong-Cha,

There will always be losses in life. Losses that can never be fully replaced. Losing you has been the most difficult thing I've ever had to deal with. I wasn't prepared to say goodbye. I wasn't prepared to let you go. I would give anything to have just one more day and one more second. But I've come to believe in unconditional love. Some bonds are unbreakable. Because even if you're not physically present, your heart is there.

It is still alive within me. Your heart is in mine. I keep it with me on days when I discover something new. I keep it with me on days when beauty appears in the most unexpected places. I keep it with me on days when I muster the strength to mend and grow. I always have it with me.

We'll meet again someday, and we won't be separated by time or place. But until then, I'll take comfort in knowing you're still with me. Your heart is secure inside mine. Some hearts are simply meant to be together, and nothing can ever change that. I adored you back then. I am in love with you right now. It was always the case. Will always be. Forever in my thoughts. I will carry you in my heart.

Every day that I miss you is another day that I fall deeper. Missing you reminds me of how much I value you. Hearing your voice and seeing your smile instantly alleviates the pain. Every kiss is a smile waiting to happen. I adore you, and you're worth the trip. I know we'll be together one day, and distance will be a thing of the past.

— Hyun-Bin

When my tears fall onto the paper, I realize I am crying out of remorse. An overwhelming sense of remorse that I can never fully express. My stomach clenched upon seeing this letter, the words, and the way he expressed himself.

As this unexpected feeling of remorse reappears and sinks into my bones, I sit motionless at my desk, staring at the letter he wrote for me. I'm not sure how long it has been since I sat down. Aera is still in the shower, so I didn't take too long.

How long did he waited for me? I am outside, hurrying through the streets with my handbag when I suddenly realize something.

I had been running for around thirty minutes since I left our apartment. It's drizzling outside; the rain has turned to mist. I can hardly see anything in front of me. My clothes got wet from the run, but that doesn't worries me.

Hyun-Bin's residence is up there somewhere. I have to visit him at least once and apologize for not coming today and for being such a bad person.

Childhood memories plays in my head. I don't know where he lives, and no one is around to inquire. I sprint down the street, calling his name. Before I even realize it, I break into another run and slip.

The rain started pouring as I tried to get up, but I couldn't seem to move a muscle. So, I don't bother. I just sit there on the sidewalk and get completely soaked as the sky pours down.

I run a hand through my wet hair. My clothes are completely soaked. I take a few deep breaths to relax and glance around. No one is out here. I set my bag aside and settled in that place.

I approach to check the time. So, I grab my phone out. By that time, someone's hand had approached my shoulder. I turned and found out it is Hyun-Bin.

"Hey" The sound of his voice floods me with mixed emotions.

"Hyun-Bin" I say, as I try to stand again but, I can't.

He take me in his arms and ask why I am here. His grip is all over my body. I'm at a loss for words. I only said, "Let me down or you'll get wet too," However, he refused to release his hold on me and tightened his grip. He wraps his fingers around my waist and begins walking.

"Where are we going?" I ask.

"To our place" he reply.

Our place? I am blushing. I bury my face in his warm and huge chest and smell him as he walks me to his place.

Thirteen
Bong-Cha

The wet white T-shirt clings to his body as water droplets run down his glistening muscles and abs. A single drop of water falls from his damp hair and lands on his muscular chest. I can almost see his body through the white T-shirt. I try not to stare and divert my attention.

The rain and his half-naked body had just enticed me to do something stupid.

"We have arrived. This is our place," he says. We are both almost dripping wet.

"Our place?" I exclaim.

"Yeah, from now on," his warm voice met my ears, and this made me uncontrollable. Lifting me and holding me tightly, he brings me closer to him. His breath and gaze explores every inch of me.

And finally, vanishes when it meets my lips. He let me sit on the couch. I said, "I'm wet," but he didn't seem to be bothered by it.

I'm completely soaked. My hair is sticking to my cheeks and neck. Raindrops running down my face in little beads. I notice him gazing at me as if he couldn't look away.

"Can you get something to change?" I interrupt and briefly break his gaze. He nodded, went inside, and came back with a sweatshirt, saying, "I turned on the heater. Go take a shower."

I reluctantly agreed and entered his room. I close the door behind me and started breathing heavily. I never imagined such a thing happening with him; I'm terrified. Perhaps I should warm up and change clothes first.

I open the door and glance at him; he has already changed and I miss seeing his exposed skin, which is now completely covered by his sweatshirt. When I notice him waiting for me for so long, I ask, "Did I take too long?"

"No, not really," he says.

His sweatshirt reached to my mid-thigh. It is too long and it covers my shorts underneath.

"I can't stop staring at you, all over you," he says, flirting in his warm voice.

"The hoodie is a little big, though," I reply.

"Are you hungry? Should we order something or?" he paused.

"Or what?" I wonder.

"You should know that I can cook. I can cook for you," he explains. His voice was slightly low.

"Do you really cook? I'd appreciate it if you could cook for me," I exclaim. He carries me into the kitchen and guides me there. Made me sit at the counter. When I watch him cook, he mentions that it's his dream to cook for someone he cares about. And I'm fortunate to have a boy who cooks for me. He's making soup for us, a soup made with Korean soybean paste. It smells great and is more suitable for rainy weather.

After we finished our soup, I assisted him with the dishes. And we sit down on the couch.

He inquired, "Should we watch something?"

"No, I'm not a big movie fan. I'm sorry," I murmur as he enters his room and returned with books.

"These will help you pass the time," he handed them to me. All of those novels are in my genre, and several of them are written by my favourite author.

"How do know?" My eyes widen. "How do you know that I love books?" I smile with delight. He remained utterly mute. I can hear the rain falling and his breath. It's grating.

I return the books to him and state, "I am not in the mood to read."

"What do you want to do?" he asks, grabbing them and setting them aside.

"I think you should say whatever you want to," I murmur, rubbing my palms against his. This is getting worse but in a good way.

"I want to kiss you, badly. Wrap my lips around yours, kiss you long enough for you to realize I'm the one," he expressed his thoughts.

I lean into him. His gaze never left mine. His hands begin to examine my carvings. Still centimetres between his and mine. He approaches, and he draws me in and grabs my hands. Our lips met. As moist as I had imagined. Wet and warm. I part my lips and let his tongue enter. I can taste his minty flavour once again. Our tongues made contact. Time had frozen our lips for nearly twelve minutes. I couldn't help but feel my blood pressure rise as a result of the passionate kiss. I run my hands over his muscular chest. He gazes at my lips, which are still moist from the kiss.

His gaze is drawn to my body. Slowly approaching my neck, he exhales a breath that sends shivers down my spine. His lips move to the right side of my neck. He let his tongue out and tasted it passionately until it reached my collarbone. He crept under the sweatshirt slowly.

I need him, so I lean in close to his ears and start teasing him with my tongue. He lets out a moan, just as I did. He raises his attention to mine and murmurs, "Take this off."

I didn't hesitate a second before removing his shirt. All I can do is bury my face in his embrace and kiss him as passionately as I can.

I kissed his chest and lower abdomen slowly, and he kept looking at me. He is so powerless that all he can do is stare at me. I undid his trousers and raised my eyes to look at him. I sit up and take off my hoodie. He didn't say anything as he grabbed my hand and lifted me into the room. He lays me down on the bed and his eyes and tongue explores every inch of mine. He savour every curve and cut of mine. I fought a little and eventually gave up.

When his lips are against my inner thighs, I moan and wrap my legs around him. I moaned as loudly as I could. He then raises his sight to my breast. I kiss his forehead as he buries his face in my chest.

"Do you want to do that?" he asks.

"I thought you shouldn't have to ask permission," I begin. He turns his eyes and kisses my thigh, licks them passionately, and finally tastes me. I can't stop moaning while he does. I take deep breaths.

"I don't have condom," he said.

"Who cares?" I reply.

And then I found myself on my back, with him on top of me. "You sure?" he questions as he spreads my legs.

After a few minutes, our bodies collided and we made love. He wouldn't release his grip on my bare skin. His fingers would never abandon me. He kissed me until he couldn't anymore. We had lost track of time and space.

Two hours later...

I'm lying in bed, and he's not here. I am completely fatigued. When he entered in me, he said, "We can't be apart. Our souls, yours and mine, are the same."

I stand up and lean back, noticing that I am dressed. Maybe he should dress me once I've exhausted. I insist on wearing the same hoodie. I walk outside to look for him, and there he is, standing on the balcony. Smoking while enjoying the rain.

"You awake?" he inquires.

"Yeah," I reply.

"I didn't know you smoke," I say hesitantly. When he sees my reaction, he drops it.

"Yes, I am a smoker. I kinda got addicted to this after my mom's death," he explained. "Don't you let me smoke?" he asks.

"Stop smoking, instead take my breath," I say as I approach, gently placing my hands on his neck and kissing him. He snatched me, lifted me, and kissed me back. He kissed me and said, "I promise I won't smoke again."

"Are you serious?" I ask.

"Yeah, I have you, my drug," he says, and I kiss him back.

I like how he addressed me. My Drug♥

Fourteen
Bong-Cha

We lay close to each other, his fingers still circling my navel. Brushing on my skin slowly. He moves his fingers down my pantie, brushing them against it, and says, "Do you remember me?"

I approach him. My lips on his neck, I slowly exhale as my lips touch his neck "Of course, of course, I do," I reply.

"Why didn't you approach me?" he wondered, his hands sinking deeper.

"I thought you had someone else in your life," I say as his fingers dig deep inside me.

"You know, I've been wanting to approach you since the first semester, but something inside me always held me back," he confesses, his fingers gently caressing me without any hesitation.

"I learn everything about you, your favourite books, songs, and everything about you. I've spent my days watching you smile from afar," he adds, dragging his hands out.

I roll around and look for my bag, which is on the side table. I picked it up and looked for the letter I had written him before he left me when we were kids. I hand it to him. He's perplexed and asks, "What's this?"

"I wrote this for you before you left me," I explain.

He gently flipped the paper and begin reading the letter, the letter I really wanted him to read. I read this almost every night and memorize every word I wrote. But it sounds much more sweet and charming when he reads those messages in his loving voice.

Dear Hyun-Bina,

I Love you so much. You have given me everything that I want. I really can't believe it, to think that you're rude. Do you really know how much I love you? Believe it. In all my life, I have never adored someone as much as I adore you. You were with me when my parents were busy with their work. I spent more time with you and your family than with mine. In all my life, I never thought I would be this happy. I am your one and only. I hope that we will have many more memorable and happy moments together in the future. To the moon and back, I adore you.

- Bong-Cha

When he finishes reading the last line, I repeat it back to him: "To the moon and back, I adore you."

He observes me blushing out of embarrassment and love. He fixed his focus on me for a moment. Then he kept the letter in a small box. He approaches me, grabs me into his arms, and says, "You loved me more, and I left you without even saying goodbye. So, it's my turn now, and I'm not going to give up."

Time flew by, and it was almost 9:00 p.m. when I checked my phone and discovered nearly ten missed calls from Aera. What bothers her so much that she called me this many times?

I didn't hesitate; I unlocked my phone and dialled her number again. She answered the phone after a few rings and said, "Hello," as the words flew out of her mouth.

"Is everything okay with you, Aera?" I inquire sceptically.

"I'm Dalia. Aera is with her mom. Aunt is returning home tonight. That's why I called you and you didn't answer," she begins.

"Where on earth are you?" she inquires.

"Actually, I'm with Hyun-Bin. When is she going to leave? I'll be there in fifteen minutes," I state.

"We have already arrived at the train station. Come right here. Aunt's train is at 9:45, and she expressed a strong desire to visit you," she tells me.

"All right, I'll be there on time," I say before hanging up the phone.

I gather my belongings and take all the books he had previously given me. But I left him a book to read.

"Um_____,

My drug, I don't read," he states.

"It is Pride and Prejudice, and I would even reject Prince Charming if he doesn't read books," I say with a smile.

I thought he would avoid reading and give me the book back, but he did the opposite. "If reading makes my drug happy, I'll spend the rest of my life doing it," he whispers while kissing my forehead.

"Are you going to leave? I assumed you would stay tonight," he continues.

"No, I actually thought the same thing, but Aera's mother is returning today. So, I guess I should go send her off," I state.

"How about I drop you off there, pick you up, and then we can both come back here to have some snacks, watch a movie, and enjoy a romantic night?" he suggests, pouting his lips with a puppy-dog expression.

"Aww, Hyun-Bin, how can I say no when you ask so sweetly?" I respond by kissing his chest.

He drives me to the train station, and we arrive at around 9:30 p.m. I noticed Aera's mother and my friends seated on the bench.

When Aera sees me, she cries, "Where have you gone?"

"I'm sorry, I was with him," I say, pointing to Hyun-Bin, who bows and greets Aera's mother. He also winked at Aera and made a thank-you gesture.

We are sitting close to Aera's mother, who is brushing my hair. "I'll miss you and Bong-Cha," she says. Then she asked me to look after Aera as well.

"Don't worry, Aunt. I'll take care of her," I say, smiling.

It's getting close to her time. The train will arrive at our station in a matter of minutes. I see Aera crying, which is something I don't see her do very often. I know she misses her family, especially her father. She sobs, and her mother gently wipes away her tears.

When the train arrived at the station, she got inside. She waved her hands and said goodbye to everyone.

"I'm really going to miss you, especially your food," Dalia shouts. As the train goes quicker, she vanishes from our sight.

When I turn to face Hyun-Bin, he smiles and says, "You should stay with Aera. She needs you right now. I can drop all of you at your houses," he offers.

That's true, I should stick with Aera for now. She is a vulnerable young girl, and I cannot leave her by herself. I nod, and we all walk up to his car.

On the way back home, we listen to music. Songs and Dalia's wit improve Aera's mood. She joined with us, and we had a good time.

Finally, when we arrive at our place, Hyun-Bin kisses me on the lips and murmurs, "Good night, Drug."

"Oh my God, what on earth is going on here? This is unbearable for me. Are you two dating?" she shouted, disgusted.

"Yeah," he says as he leans in and kisses me again.

"Bong-Cha, you mentioned you were at his place recently. What did you guys do? Did you two had sex at his place?" she inquired.

"Stop, Dalia," I shouted out of humiliation.

"Yeah, and she's mine from now on," he replied, kissing me again.

"Enough, guys," I shout again as I follow Aera inside.

Fifteen
Aera

Everything is changing in this day and age. If we don't pay attention to it on a daily basis, we may not realize that everything around us has changed. When we look back in time, people you thought would be there forever aren't, and people you never thought you'd be chatting with are now some of your closest friends.

Life makes little sense, and as we grow older, it will make even less sense.

I'm all alone in my room. We used to eat dinner together. Everything has changed recently. Bong-Cha spends much of her time with Hyun-Bin and Dalia, so she isn't as close to me as before.

We go to college together, she has been sitting with him since they started dating. The seat next to me remains unoccupied. I eat alone and go back home alone. Hyun-Bin has been picking her up after our classes every day and dropping her off at home at 9:30. They eat dinner together, so I don't get to chat with her at night.

Dalia and I finish our dinner and go back to our room. Time had a significant impact on Bong-Cha, separating her from me. The challenging aspect is that she is completely unaware that she is ignoring me.

I spent the entire day with the man I met months ago. He is a decent man and a supporter of mine. After college, we spent the entire day in the park or at the museum. He makes a few caustic remarks that are highly relatable to my life. That is what makes our bond even stronger. When life becomes difficult, God will send someone to help us. That's exactly what he is to me. His words heal me as if he were a Band-Aid.

I used to walk down this path with my friends. The cool breeze blowing on me, the fresh air smelling good, and the sun peeking through the clouds made them appear like orange cotton candy. These things around never changed, so why did people?

It feels ridiculous to spend time with an unfamiliar man. I sometimes wonder if I've gone insane. How can I spend the entire evening with someone I hardly know? I don't know what he does, where he lives, or even his name. I can't seem to get away from him. He has something.

"Hello, Aera," a warm voice says.

"Yeah, how did you find me?" I'm curious about how he discovered me, since I didn't even approach him. I am at the back.

"I know," he begins. I'm used to it. He always notices my presence. And today, I discovered that he can detect my presence too.

"I want to get to know you."

"Know me? My story isn't very interesting," he reasoned.

"Well, what's in that notebook?" I often see him engrossed in his notebook. So, I'm intrigued.

"Something I don't want to forget," he sighs.

"What exactly does that mean?" I'm sceptical.

"Everything changes in life, Aera. When time passes, it can even take away your memories. All of my beautiful memories are fading away," he burst into tears.

"Those are about your love, right?" I pursued the matter further.

"Yes," he says, his eyes welling up with tears, and when they land on his lap, I rub his hands and console him.

"How does she look like?" I inquire.

"She's like a dark sky," he exclaims.

"A dark sky?" I inquire.

"I shone because she made me shine. I want to be her star. I want to show her the various stages of my love. As stars do for the infinite sky." He is in pain, he grins.

"Is she still alive?" I'm not supposed to ask this. Damn it, my stupid mouth.

"Yeah, she lives in my heart," he said, setting the journal aside and turning to face me.

I'm not sure how a man can love someone so deeply. Someone like him is rare in a world of betrayal and deception.

"What's inside the notebook?"

"Our tale, Aera. It is our story. Memories are slipping away from me, and I've even forgotten my own name. All I can think of is you and this place," he elaborated.

My gaze wanders around the notebook. What would his story be? I am curious. I'm intrigued by his story.

Everything goes silent, and then, as I expected, a beep sound reaches my eardrums and travels back. My blood pressure rises, and my legs and hands begin to quiver.

People noticing me in this way made me uneasy, so I collected my belongings and ran away from him. "Aera_____," he shouts as his voice approaches and my legs tremble.

I sprinted as quickly as I could, but then I felt my nose start to bleed and it spilled all over my collar. I'm wiping my blood with my sleeve. It keeps flowing, just like the sound within me. I couldn't take the anguish any longer, so I leaned on my palms to keep myself from collapsing.

People are staring at me as if I'm crazy, and I don't want to be here. I try to move, but I can't. I give up, lying on the roadside footpath, covering my ears with my hands and yelling.

"Enough, Enough,

Enough, Enough, Enough, Enough, Enough, Enough,
Enough, Enough, Enough, Enough, Enough, Enough,
Enough, Enough, Enough, Enough, Enough, Enough,
Enough, Enough, Enough, Enough, Enough, Enough,
Enough, Enough, Enough, Enough, Enough, Enough,
Enough, Enough, Enough, Enough, Enough, Enough,
Enough, Enough, Enough, Enough, Enough, Enough,
Enough, Enough, Enough, Enough, Enough, Enough,
Enough, Enough, Enough, Enough, Enough, Enough,
Enough, Enough, Enough, Enough, Enough, Enough,
Enough, Enough, Enough, Enough, Enough, Enough,
I can't tolerate anymore. I am exhausted.

I wake up to find myself on bed. I'm wrapped in a bed cover and sleeping in someone else's bed. I'm not sure where I am.

I can barely remember what happened before I blacked out. All I remember is screaming and recognizing someone staring at me. Apart from that, I can't think of anything else. How did I get here? Who assisted me? I don't even know what time it is.

I awake from my sleep and exited the room. I noticed a woman performing rituals and chanting something that I don't understand.

"Excuse me? I apologize for interrupting, but where am I?"

"You're at my place, Aera," she says.

"How do you know my name?" My mouth drops open.

"I am a fortune teller. I can perceive things that you cannot." She sounds unintelligent.

"You should check your health," she advises.

"I should," I agree.

"Lately, I've been experiencing some issues, and I've been noticing strange things." I begin.

"Come sit here," she says. I follow her instructions.

She instructs me to cross my legs and sit upright. She then spells something while holding my hands. "Time makes you understand everything," she continues. "And you're going to face something you don't even understand. Just be strong enough to accept everything," she says as she lets go of my hands.

"I don't understand," I admit.

"I told you, you don't get it. Let time teach you everything," she begins. I check my watch and it is 8:30 p.m. Unconsciously, I have spent over two hours in a stranger's home. Time continues to play tricks on my life.

When I left her house, she smiled and said "You're about to face the most difficult part of life. Be careful," I hug her and bid her goodbye.

I ring the bell when I arrive at my home. Nobody dares to open the door. I got in by using a spare key. It's dark in here, and no one has arrived.

Sometimes I think I'm happy. When I'm with my friends, I burst into laughter, throwing my head back and covering my mouth. But then the day becomes night. My carefree grin gives way to unfathomable melancholy.

I lay in bed, contemplating all the things I wished I could say. I am cheerful and sometimes depressed, extroverted yet shy, exuberant but also quiet. But I'm mostly empty.

Sixteen
Aera

The time is eleven in the morning when I wake up. It's almost noon. I made a mistake and missed my class. Why don't they at least try to wake me up?

I tried to get out of bed, but my legs didn't cooperate. I am exhausted and feeling dizzy as well. When I approach the kitchen, I find a sticky note on the refrigerator.

Hi, Aera take rest. I prepared food.

Check the oven. Stay at home and let's talk in the evening.

- Bong-Cha ☺

I checked the oven; she made me rice porridge and sandwiches too. Which she kept warm in a hot pack. My stomach is grumbling from the delicious aroma and hunger. I quickly brushed my teeth and freshened up, then grabbed two sandwiches for myself. I also had some mayonnaise for dipping.

When I take the first bite and chewed, it tastes terrible. My tongue detects a bitter flavour. I can't eat that. What happens to my tongue? I place my hands on my neck to check my temperature, and I am burning up.

I am with fever. I notice and pull the porridge from the oven and take a few spoonful into my mouth. Yeah, it's better for my sensitive palate.

My stomach can't tolerate the porridge; I vomit in the living room. I can't stop myself from vomiting. I smell bad. I'm also feeling dizzy.

Then I clean everything up by myself. And then I go to take a shower.

After a whole twenty minutes of showering, I find myself warm and better. I got into bed and tried to eat something again because I needed to take tablets. I tried to eat the remaining porridge while taking two pills for fever and nausea.

I pulled out my phone and found a few notifications from Bong-Cha.

Bong Cha: I want to talk.

Bong Cha: I'll be there at five, stay home.

I'm not staying at home. What's the point? She didn't even care about my existence since she started dating, and now she's acting as if she does. At five, I want to meet him though.

I randomly accessed our university chat group and came across images of myself and the man I spent time with. What exactly is going on? I'm perplexed.

There have been talks and comments about me being in a relationship with that man. And that photo is from yesterday when I comforted him by rubbing his hands while he cried.

"Nonsense" I murmur out of frustration and disgust. So, I am going to spend my time on Instagram Reels. I received nearly 50 messages from random profiles when I opened the app, and many people tagged me in comments and posts.

What the hell is going on? There are pictures of the old man and me. Few of us are actually sitting next to each other. And the remaining posts are disgusting. They morphed my photos and his photos with random porn.

I scrolled through every post until I found something that made me cry: a random image of a porn star with my face morphed onto it, accompanied by the hashtags #Aerawhore and #Aeraporn.

People are tagging me in comments and having strange conversations like this,

Unknown 1: She's clearly a whore.

Unknown 2: She did the same thing to me.

Unknown 1: Really? What a nasty whore.

Out of humiliation, I shiver. How can they talk about me in this manner? My body is shivering as a result of their discussions about me. They're talking shit about me by tagging me. A few people are tagging me and asking me to make them happy as well.

How do people just randomly talk shit about someone they barely know? This man is a good friend of mine and now I'm feeling embarrassed. How can I ever face him?

I'm at a loss for what to do; a few people have commented that it's a fake photo that has been morphed, but no one is listening. Human beings spend their time on trivial matters and engage in gossip about others.

Shame and humiliation cause me to clench my knees and scratch my legs. Nobody is coming to help. It's all about me, and who cares? My eyes started tearing up, and I couldn't stop. I wrapped myself in the bed cover and buried myself in the bed.

My only thought is, "How can I face people after this? What if they ask me to make them happy or to send them my nudes?" I dash my head in the cot and cry loudly.

"No, no, God I can't stand this,

Please_____,"

I doze out by crying.

My eyesight became blurry when I tried to open my eyes slowly. I can't see anything. I rubbed my eyes, and all I could see was my friend's face. Everyone is sitting around me as if they are at my funeral. Yang-Min and Hyun-Yang smile at me and wrap their arms around me when I open my eyes.

"Everything will be fine. Don't worry, baby," they say quietly. I noticed Tae-Moon working on his laptop and wondered what he is doing there. Yeah, he's a good friend of mine, but we're not that close.

Hyun-Bin is on a bean bag on my left side, and I notice him. He's looking at me. He opens his arms and says, "Come" when I meet his gaze. I rush up to him and hug him. He gently caresses my back and shoulder. I burst into tears and started sobbing. He dragged me away and said, "We're not going to let anyone hurt you, okay? We're here for everything" he wiped my tears.

"Where have Bong-Cha and Dalia gone?" I inquire, wiping my tears away and taking a deep breath.

"They're in the kitchen making coffee for all of us," he explains.

Bong-Cha returns with coffee and hurries to me when she sees that I am awake. I expect her to chastise me for being so careless and for engaging in conversation with a stranger. But she did the opposite, hugging me and inviting Dalia to join us. Our regular trio hug. We haven't hugged like this in a long time.

With the right people, even pain becomes painless. My friends are my pain relievers.

"I am sorry Aera, lately I didn't took proper care of you. It's all my responsibility, and I had no idea you were going through such hardships. Please accept my heartfelt apologies." She places her hands on mine, and her tears fell onto them.

"What is he doing here?" I gesture towards Tae-Moon with my fingers.

"I am deleting all of your photos. Almost deleted everything, only a few left," he smiled and continued his work.

"You shouldn't stay in this room all day, Aera. I think you should come out," the Yangs tried to console me.

"No, I don't think it's the right time. At the very least, I need one more day to get over this," I begin.

"No, staying here implies that you accept those things. You should act normally," Hyun-Bin states and others concur.

"You make an excellent point," Bong-Cha adds.

"How about going to Karaoke and having a good time?" Tae-Moon proposes, and the others agrees.

They all are standing around waiting for me to get ready. Actually, I'm not in the mood for karaoke or any kind of fun. I want to be alone. And they are assuming that if I stay alone, I'll become more depressed. Well, that's true, though.

When we head to the Karaoke, there are several individuals who stalk me on campus and social media. They are the people who manipulated my photos. I'm disgusted, and I'm fucking enraged at them.

"Did you see who's here? Our lovely whore," one among them admits. My nerves are twitching. If they say one more word again, they're dead.

"Little whore," they giggle.

I drag my hands across to punch them in their face. But Tae-Moon and Hyun-Bin did that before I approached them. They both punched those nasty guys, and one of them ended up with a purple circle on his face, while the other one was bleeding. Dalia grabs his hair and pulls out a few strands from his head. They are screaming in horror. I enjoy seeing my friends standing up for me.

"You dirty bitch, watch your mouth," Hyun-Yang told the person who called me a whore by kicking his huge ass and dick. His eyes are about to close, and he shouts loudly while covering his groin with his two hands.

They made them, kneel in front of me, and order them to apologize.

"Sorry, whore," the other says before being hit on the back of the head by Bong-Cha.

"We're sorry, but what we said is the truth," one of them laughs at me.

I'm enraged, so I lift his head and ask, "What's true? Tell me," I demand.

"The man, about your relationship. He's a stalker. He frequently follows you, and his intention is solely for you. He wants you and you need money so, you're fucking him" he admits.

"He's a good man, he's not a stalker. And watch your tongue before talking nonsense about me" I yell and give a bang on his head.

"Go out and look around, you'll definitely find him along the crowd. If his intentions are good, why would he follows you?" he wonders.

I am blank. I'm at a loss for words. I saw him everywhere I went, including the park and the museum, and my mother also spoke with him at the market. Is he truly a stalker? I'm perplexed.

I hurried out and looked for him. It's seven o'clock in the evening, and this route is busy. This street is bustling with activity. Restaurants are filled with students, while bars are frequented by adults. Parents are walking their children.

And I look around for him. "I don't want to see you in this crowd, please. I don't want you to be a stalker," I murmur to myself.

And our gazes connect until my gaze is drawn to a lamppost across the street. My eyes filled up with tears as I saw him standing far away and staring at me. He waves his hands and smiles. I rush up to him and approach him. When I get close to him, he exclaims, "Hi Aera," with a big smile on his face.

"Why are you here?" I sound impolite.

"Just a walk," he responded sceptically.

"Don't lie," I cry, as he steps forward, facing his toes and avoiding eye contact.

"Take a look at me, mister. Are you a stalker? You're interested in me, aren't you?" I scream. People are staring at me like I'm crazy.

"Please say no," I keep muttering to myself.

He didn't respond, "I want to tell you something. Please let me explain," he continue.

"Answer me. I don't wanna hear your rubbish. Just answer me," I yell once more.

He goes silent for almost a couple of minutes and says, "Yes, I am."

I slapped him. Yeah, literally, I did.

Actually, I had no intention of offending him. I trusted him, but he duped me throughout our time together. I can't resist this. I shared everything with him, even about my childhood and Hyun-Bin, but he lied to me.

People are gathered around us, watching me yelling at him. What is it with these people? They do nothing when someone asks for help, but they dedicate all of their time to something like this. They're fucking insane.

"I thought you were a good person. In Karaoke, I defended for you. When you're with me, you always manage to trick me. You are a liar. You don't know all the hardships I've been going through. You just let my hopes down. You let me down," I yell at him, and Bong-Cha drags me back.

She draws me in and whisper, "People are watching Aera, Let's just leave this place and stop talking about it. Okay?" I agree, and we all head to our places.

Seventeen
Aera

I don't hear anything beyond that.

The way he said, yes.

My head starts to feel increasingly pressured. My stomach and my heart. I sit on the edge of the sofa and look down at the ground. I take a quick breath in and then exhale as soon as he returns with the coffee. Tae-Moon is standing in front of me, with his feet practically touching mine. When his arm comes down, he places the coffee aside and wraps it around me. The entire time, I cry, and he hugs me.

I'm solely to blame. I should not have allowed him to get close to me. I did this to myself.

"Did you know before?" he asks, his fingers running through my hair.

"I anticipated him being an amazing friend and well-wisher, but ___." I resume my silence. He give me a cozy hug and pats my back.

Tae-moon lives and resides alone in his apartment instead of sharing a home with his parents. He is a trustworthy hacker. When he was thirteen, his parents abandoned him. He had a job at a computer centre and taught himself software skills. He created a children's program when he was only eighteen, and it is currently the most popular children's application in South Korea.

He's quite wealthy and only enrols in college to pass the time while he's free. Though absurd, that is the situation.

He turns to face me and says, "Coffee." "Yeah, I forgot," I reply as I take a sip of the enticing aroma. When I had my first sip, I felt revitalized.

"How's it?" he enquire, excited.

"Perfect" I say.

He smiled at me and moved to the kitchen. "Are you hungry?"

I shake my head. I wouldn't be able to eat even if I could. I entered the kitchen. When I walk in, he is switching between the oven and the counter. "I thought you were hungry," he says, looking up at me.

"I am."

He asked me to wait for him, so I did. He reappears, carrying two bowls of noodles and kimchi. It's almost too beautiful to eat, and it smells fantastic. When I take a bite, I realize that it's the best kimchi noodles I've ever had.

"Can I ask you a favour?" I ask.

"Sure, anything." He states.

"I want to visit a place, I mean I want to go somewhere. It has been three days since the incident, but I still see that man attempting to approach me. So, I would like you to take me there. I'm terrified to go alone." I explain.

"There's no need for explanations; I can do anything that you require," he states.

"Where do you want to go?" he asks.

"I ran into a lady. She works as a fortune teller." I say.

He sighs and looks at me for a moment. Then he laughed and asked, "Do you believe these things?"

The manner in which he inquired is revolting, yet it is true. Who believes such nonsense? Even I don't believe in concepts like fortune, fate, destiny, and so on... I am more pragmatic. I couldn't help but feel perplexed. Since the day I met him, things have become more confusing.

"Yeah, I am" I spit out and keep quiet.

He pauses for a few moments before grabbing my hands and saying, "Let's go." We use the lift to go to his parking spot. It's quiet as we walk in. Totally silent, just him and me. I receive a lot of looks. He attempts to make eye contact more often, but I often try to avoid it. When his gaze wanders all over me, I get goose bumps.

I have no idea what love is. How people feel and how they find their match. All I know is that this man standing close to me is interested in me. I like him, but I'm not ready to fall in love.

He kept staring at me, his eyes moving from my toes to my hair. When he finally stopped staring at my chest,

I instinctively crossed my hands across it. "God! Why are these boys always the same? When will we arrive at the parking lot?" I mutter under my breath.

"What?" he asks.

"Did he hear what I said?" I freeze in amazement. Shit no____ I'm speechless; all I can do is stare into his eyes.

He just glances back and approaches close, tilting his head and slipping his hands to my right shoulder. As he leaned in, I thought he was going to kiss me, so I instinctively pushed him away and used my hands to cover my mouth.

"No, no. You misjudged me, Aera," his voice trembles with embarrassment. "I was just trying to remove the thread from your coat," he continues. His cheeks are flushed, and his eyes are filled with humiliation.

"Shit._____"

Aera, you should keep your thoughts to yourself. Take a look at what you did. I hit myself on the head for my insane behaviour. I approach him and say, "I am sorry. That's not supposed to happen. I mistook your approach for a kiss."

"Yeah, yeah... okay," he says, still embarrassed.

Finally, after all of this confusion, we arrive at the parking lot. As we approach his car, he open the door and let me sit down first. Then he walks in, starts the car, and asks, "With your permission, may I do your seat belt? Or else you'll think I'm trying to kiss you."

"Shit___

Look, that's a mistake, okay?

You're mean, Tae-Moon," I yell out of humiliation.

The entire journey is too quiet. He didn't even looked at me once. His whole focus is on the road and the steering wheel. His hands are firm and veiny; perhaps he exercises regularly. I try to strike up a polite chat, but nothing works, and I'm a little hesitant. My eyes are fixed on him; I continue to stare at him, and when he turns beside me, I quickly shift my gaze elsewhere.

"What happened?" he asked.

"What? Nothing," I say as I look out of the window.

"Why are you so silent today? Is that me? Or is that the kiss? What's troubling you?" he asks again.

"I told you, it's nothing," I say.

"No, you're lying. It cannot be nothing," he insist.

"It's about the incident, Tae-Moon. That dude, I can't believe he did this. And the fortune teller_____ I have no idea what's going on in my life."

"Let's simply forget about that night and that elderly man. Then what's with this fortune teller? I know you're not one of those people who believes everything."

"I know I seem silly, but that lady stated I am going to have the most difficult time of my life, and I believe it has already begun."

"I'm at a loss for words, but I'll be there for you in any situation. All you have to do is believe me. That's all there is to it." He smiles.

I place my hand on his lap, and he places his left hand over mine. I didn't care about anything at the time. We only had our hands together. The way his hand presses against mine and the warmth it provides is heavenly.

"I'm in love," he says.

"What? Really? With whom?" I ask.

"All I can think of is you, and beyond you, I can't see anything." He says this as his voice warms and his hands massages my hands.

"I love you too, but___" I remain mute, and no one opened the dialogue. So I begin, "I kinda feel like I belong to someone else. I regard you as a good friend."

"Who? To whom do you belong?" His voice gets hard, almost too hard. I can see the sadness in his eyes. It hurts to hurt him. I don't want to cause him any harm.

"Either I don't know, or I don't know to whom I belong. It's somebody___

Someone else owns me."

"I understand. I'm not pressuring you to adore me, Aera. Love should be mutual." He continues. And when he responded, Love should be mutual, my lungs locked up the oxygen I inhaled. I can hardly breathe, my eyes are half-dozen, and that familiar sound is playing in my brain. I can barely see anything except for those visions.

"Stop, stop!" I yell, dazed and anguished.

Eighteen
Aera

I exhale a rasping breath and notice a light behind my closed eyelids. I force my eyes open to behold the vibrant colours. I'm perplex and afraid. I find myself caught between reality and my illness. When I open my eyes, there is nothing to see. So, I close my eyes once again. Then, I start rubbing my hands on my stomach and cleaning the blood off the ground. I hear a deep sound. Incomprehensible. Awful sound.

The sound slowly fades, and I can barely hear someone chanting my name, Aera. It repeats once, twice, and three times. Then someone lifts my face and gently taps it. I struggle to open my eyes, but my frail body is not cooperating. And I meet his gaze as I open my eyes slightly. The identical eyes I saw before I dozed off.

"Aera! Aera, what's happening with you? Please wake up and look at me," I barely hear his voice.

I find myself standing in a field, a battlefield. All I can see is myself and nothing else. I had never felt anything like this before. It's absolutely nothing. I start walking in the direction I am facing, and I continue walking until everything disappears. There is no destination, and I have no idea where I am going. The breeze gently caresses my skin and permeates my pores like a delicate needle. I'm fatigue, and my legs begin to tremble with each step I take. I sit on the floor once again.

Misty droplets drip and settle on my face. I'm gradually getting over my dizziness, and I can see light shining through my closed eyelids. I'm finally able to move my arms. Slowly, I open my eyes and see him. He appears to be in a state of worry and concern. When I open my eyes, he grabs me with his bare hands and pulls me close to his muscular chest. His heartbeat is audible to me. It's as if his heart is pounding in my head.

"Are you alright?"

"Yeah, I am."

"I'm fine," I insist.

"What happens to you? You're ill," he says, tears welling up in his eyes. "I can't imagine you going through this." His tears fell on my leg, so I approach to wipe them away. I approach him, and when my chest touches his, he embraces me.

I feel like I've entered a K-Drama realm because of the way he pulled me close and embraced me. I have seen such things happen in dramas.

"Don't worry, I'm fine," I say.

"No, you aren't. I saw you rubbing your stomach and yelling in pain," he say, panicking.

"Did I?" I'm sceptical.

"You did, you did. I believe we should see a doctor before going to see the fortune teller," he said.

"No, fine. I'm used to this. I could improve with medication" I say ridiculously.

"Are you sure about that?" He inquires.

He drives me to the nearest convenience store. I open my door to follow him out, but he urges me to stay in the car and asks, "Is there anything else you need?"

"Nothing, just pills," I say.

He returns with tablets, a water bottle, and a strawberry milkshake. He opens the bottle and dispenses the pills. I swallow each tablet one by one, and as I reach the last one, he gently brushes my chest to help it go down. My body feels cold.

"Drink this," he hands me the strawberry milk and goes to start the car.

Blushing from shyness; I try not to show it, but my dumb face turns a shade of pink. I turn to face the window, my hair covering my face.

"There is no need to cover your face. I already saw you," he laughs.

"What?' I mutter, "Shit..."

We arrive at the location in ten minutes. I grab his hands in mine and walk inside. It's almost quiet here. I can't see anyone walking down the street, and the house is too dark. There is only one light in front of the house to welcome visitors.

Tae-Moon is frightening. He's slipping out the door. "Hey, it's not a haunted house. She's a fortune teller, not a witch," I laugh.

"I don't like such things because they make me nervous," he says.

"How adorable! Who admits to being scared?" I giggle and motion for him to wait by the car.

When I finally ring the doorbell, the woman opens the door, too quickly. She grabs my hands and pulls me in. I remain completely still, not even exhaling any carbon dioxide. I just stare at the location and at her. "Why are you here?" She asks, puzzled. I assume she would figure it out. "I am a fortune teller, and I can only see a bleak future for you. I can't read your mind; you must tell me what's on your mind," she states.

"I want to see my future," I say.

"You already did; you don't need me. You can see your own future," she says.

"What?" I'm clueless.

"Time made you see what would happen and what has happened. All of your quests will be completed before your birthday. It's an omen for you. It could be a good or negative omen." And also, she says as she searches for something, "the guy you left outside is going to help you heal."

She comes to a halt, reaches into her bag, and takes out a pencil. A small pencil that appears to be antique. She hands me the pencil and says, "When you wake up, you'll have all the answers you need. At that point, connect all the pieces together, and you will understand what is happening to you."

"What about my pain? I'm experiencing excruciating pain inside my head, and an agonizing sound keeps playing," I am lament.

"Everything is predetermined. Aera, you are destined to discover the truth. You had a chance, but you blew it," she says, staring into a mirror in the room where I had previously been resting.

"What? Have I wrecked it? I'm not aware of it," I exclaim.

"What if I miss the next opportunity?" I'm asking out of anguish.

"You won't get another chance if you lose this," she says, eerily.

"I'm leaving here tomorrow. If you find yourself in a difficult situation, come to my house after you wake up and stand near this mirror. It will provide you with some clarifications," she says.

Why does she keep on saying 'after you wake'? I came here seeking clarification, but now I'm even more confused. What exactly is going on? How should I proceed? How can I wake up? Is this a dream or what? Everything stinks.

I leave, and when I reach the car, I notice something even more adorable. Tae-Moon is sleeping. "Aww, my darn eyes. How adorable is he?" I exclaim.

I get inside and slowly shut the door. I don't want to disturb him. I heard him muttering something under his breath while he is sleeping. I laugh and brush his head, but I don't know what was going on inside me. I simply approach to kiss him. My heart begins to beat as quickly as possible. When I get closer, I deny it. I stop.

Nineteen
Bong-Cha

After hearing a loud bang on the door, I rush to open it. The house is eerily quiet. Both Aera and Dalia are not at home, so it's just me and the dead silence. As I approach the doorway, the banging intensifies, and it seems like someone is urgently trying to get in.

I'm scared and bewilder right now. My friends will not pound on the door. They only ring the doorbell or call me. It scares me a lot. Who is banging on the door like this? I am sensitive to noise, and the closer I get, the drowsier I feel. So, I return to retrieve my earmuffs to protect myself.

When I reach the door and place my hands on it, I hear another knock from behind it. My hands are trembling. It's Tae-Moon, I notice as I shift my gaze through the peephole. He's knocking because of an emergency. I dash to the front door. And as soon as I opened the door, he starts yelling, "Where on earth are you?"

"I'm sorry, you should have called me instead of knocking so hard," I declare.

"I forgot to take my phone out of the car. I came here to drop off Aera, but she passed out on the way up. I had no idea what to do, so I carried her up," he elaborates.

"Where is she?" I ask anxiously.

On the right, he gestures with his hands. I look around and see Aera leaning against the wall and sitting on the floor near the steps. She is tired and hiccups constantly. She mutters something under her breath while flailing her hands around erratically.

"Is she drunk?" I burst out yelling.

"She is, indeed."

'How dare you allow her to drink? She doesn't drink and can't handle it. I won't allow her to spend time alone with you after this. What did you do to her?" I yell in frustration.

He grabs my shoulders and shakes me twice, saying, "Listen, we went to a fortune teller's house. I fell asleep while waiting for her to leave. And when I opened my eyes, I saw her fainting. I went near to see if she was drunk. I didn't make her drink. She did it all by herself."

What? I'm frozen in shock. Why is she drinking alcohol? I found myself at a loss for words and mistakenly yelled angrily at Tae-Moon. I am frozen in embarrassment. I simply let our discussion continue in silence. He stares at me for a few moments before saying, "Help me lift her."

"Oh, sure," I insist. We walk her into my room, and when she lands on the bed, she exclaims, "I have to wake up." We laugh, and I put the blanket around her while he takes off her shoes and socks.

"Change her clothes and put her to bed for a while. Don't bother her. She is experiencing a lot of unusual things. Let her rest," he states, but it feels more like he's ordering me not to disturb her.

"Okay," I insist.

He kneels down to Aera, strokes her hair, and rests his hands on her tummy, saying, "She mentioned feeling something in here. I believe she is ill. Can you take her to the hospital?"

"Sure, why not? I'll take her when she wakes up," I offer. He places a gentle kiss on her forehead and gazes at her for a few minutes. Then, he lifts his gaze to me and whispers, "Don't let her know about this kiss." I wink at him and playfully say, "Okay, donkey." He looks confused for a moment, but then he smiles and responds, "Okay, donkey."

I invite him to stay for a while, and he accepts my invitation. He keeps his gaze fixed on Aera. His complete attention is drawn to Aera's bedroom. I see concern in his eyes for her. I only receive one-word answers from him, no matter what I ask him. I put in an effort to start a conversation, but it often ends with a one-word reply. Perhaps he doesn't want to be distracted from looking at her. I suppose.

I go into the kitchen to prepare some coffee for both of us. I'm a coffee junkie, so I always have instant coffee. I prepare two mugs and approach him with them.

"Coffee," I offer.

"Yeah, thanks," he says, as I bring him the coffee. He took three large sips and places the coffee mug on the table. I detect a buzzing coming from inside his pocket. He sounds like he's farting, but he's not. It's his mobile. The phone is in vibrate mode. I smile, and he grab his phone and exit the house.

Aera is still unconscious after more than two hours. I can't help but let her sleep for a little while longer. I get up from the couch to check on Aera. Her hands are on her stomach as she sobs. She is stroking her stomach and unintentionally murmuring something. I can't hear anything. All I can say is that she is having a nightmare. I decide to wake her up. I cannot see her sobbing in sorrow.

She keeps shouting, and when I try to stop her, she screams. Her hands quiver, and the way she shouts creeps me out. I took her hands in mine and began rubbing them together to warm her up. She's shivering. I'm at a loss for what to do. Why is she so cold? I even turned on the heater.

"Oh, Aera..."

"What should I do now?"

A glass of water is on the table. I rush to grab the glass and spill all the water on her face. She let out a deep breath as I poured the water. Her lungs expellees all the oxygen she had been holding in. Her breathing is raspy. Her lungs made an unsuitable sound every time she breathe. It sounds like "zzz".

She moves her hands slowly, and her eyes react to the water I dropped on her. She finally attempts to open her eyes. "Bong-Cha," her voice cracks and reaches my ears. When I get closer, she pulls me in and whispers, "I need some fresh air," her breath tickles my ears.

"But you're already cold. You can't leave now," I say.

"It's difficult for me to breathe. Please," she begs as she clutches my hands and starts to calm down. Her temperature eventually drops.

I shrug and say, "Okay, before we go, let's get change."

"Where would you like to go?" I'm curious.

"To the park," she says quietly.

It has been almost a week. She hadn't been to the park since the moment that man confessed his feelings. The sky is cloudy, and the orange sunset makes it more colourful and stunning. Children begin to interact with their peers. Elderly people are walking and conversing. I start watching the scene, and Aera is also enjoying herself. "What a beautiful sight!" she exclaims. "Yeah, so beautiful," I say enthusiastically.

We sit on the bench beneath the large tree and took in the scenery. She is currently doing well. I can see her face turning red and her ability to walk diminishing. She abandons me and gets to play with the kids.

She closes her eyes and starts counting from one to ten, while all the other kids rush to hide before the countdown is over. A girl rushes up behind the bench where I'm seated. Aera always says that children are stress relievers. That is a well-established fact.

I go to answer a phone call from Hyun-Bin. I signal to Aera that I am going to answer a phone call. She smiles and resumes her game.

"Hello"

"Hey, my love."

"Are you free right now?" He asks with a seductive voice.

"Kinda, yeah, I am," I say.

"Shall I come over?"

"Actually, I'm at the children's park," I say, biting my bottom lip.

"You look more attractive doing this," he says.

"Do what?" I have no idea.

"Turn around," he says.

I turn and look for him. He grabs my hand and pulls me closer to him. My pupils dilate, and I raise an eyebrow, wondering, "What are you doing here?"

He takes my hands in his and wraps them around his neck. I insist, placing my hands around his neck and tightening my grip. His hands trace the curvature of my hips as he pulls me closer to him. He plants a tender, warm kiss on my neck, and as I let out a moan, he gently bites my lower lip and whispers, "I'm here for this."

"It's a children's park, so please stop. You should watch yourself," I remark as I take a step back from him. "This is me," he grabs me again. "I always need you," his rich voice seduces me. "No, not now," I answer, and he asks, "How about tonight at your place?" He tries to entice me once more. I couldn't help but agree.

I led him to the bench where I was sitting, and we took a seat. We discussed about Aera. I told him everything about her health, and then he ask, "Where is she?"

"Right there," I respond, waving my hand.

"Where?" he inquires once more.

My heart starts racing as I realize she's gone. I'm panicking and feeling overwhelmed, which is making it difficult for me to think clearly. It's as if I left my brain somewhere else. I am unable to think or act. I go around the park chanting "Aera_____"

Hyun-Bin follows me and helps me locate Aera. I come to a halt near where she was playing and I ask a child about her; she tells me that a man approached Aera and she fled.

What the hell is going on? Shit! I dash out of the park, leaving Hyun-Bin behind, and notice Aera waiting to cross the street. I gather all of my strength and yell her name, "Aera!"

She takes a step to cross the street, and when she hears my voice, she turns to face me. She stares at me for a long time. I continue on my way towards her when I notice a car speeding up on the same road where Aera is standing.

"Aera, there's a car! Look!" I yell at her while running on the opposite side of the street. The car is almost there, and as I arrive, I notice Aera falling onto the road in front of the car.

Twenty
Aera

All I sense is a brightness behind my eyes. I am unable to open my eyes. My eyes feel as if they have been glued shut. I can't close my eyes. I tried everything I could think of, but all I see when I open my eyes is white. A white ceiling, white wall, and even my clothes are all white in this room.

Except for my eyes, nothing else was responsive. I try to move my body, but eventually give up. I want to turn my head and see what's on the other side. But none of my organs are functioning; it's as if I've been paralyzed.

I muster all of my strength to pull my body up. I want to sit; my back hurts after lying in the same position for so long. I raise my hands to grab something that will help me stay awake. Then I realized that I wasn't even able to move them. They are sleeping. When I try to move, I experience a buzzing sensation throughout my entire body.

I finally raise my hands after a fifteen-minute struggle. I fold all of my fingers to see if it would work, and the first time I did, I felt a needle in the top of my hand. It's linked to a bottle of something, probably glucose.

Then I realize I am at the hospital. Slowly, my body begins to recover, and when I am finally able to sit up, I notice Bong-Cha sleeping on the couch to my right. The coach is also white. There is a window on the wall, and the sunshine is hitting my eyes directly, reminding me of what happened yesterday.

The man approached me to talk, but I declined and ran from of the park. And when I tried to cross the street, I heard Bong-Cha calling my name. Later, I realized that I was standing in the centre of the road, and a vehicle was speeding towards me. When the car's lights shone on my face, I instinctively covered my face with my hands.

My neck hurts so much I instinctively move my hands to check whether I hit smacked on the head. I reach up and touch the back of my neck and head, but as I do so, my hands accidentally hit the side table and some things fall. It produces a loud noise that wakes her up when it reaches her ears.

She run towards me only a fraction of a second after waking up. She dials the hospital's landline number as she caresses my hair.

Things are strange. People are looking at me as if I am a miracle. The doctor checks my pulse and asks me to answer a few questions. Finally, he states I am completely fine and that I should be on medication for a few months.

Visitors bringing fruits and flowers are arriving and departing one by one. "Come on, guys, I'm fine," I cry as the Yangs enter, carrying a floral bouquet. "Okay look, I don't have cancer or a tumour. I'm completely fine," they smile. After half an hour of talk, they pulled me into a warm hug.

"Please, no more sorrows," I say.

Bong-Cha respects my space by escorting all the people and then eventually enters. "Are you okay?" she asks.

"Not at all. I had this strange dream after fainting yesterday," I start.

"Yesterday? A week passed. You've been in a coma since the day you fainted," she says.

"What?" I'm freezing from shock.

"Yes, anyway, you're fine now. Just assume you've been sleeping here for a week," she insists.

"Actually, I saw something. It could have been my imagination, a dream, or something else, but it felt real," I explain.

"What?" she has no idea. She takes a seat next to me in the chair. She grabs my hands and gestures for me to continue.

After an hour...

Bong-Cha is completely stunned. She falls silent for a long period, and all she can do is attempt to say something before falling silent again. She imitates this for a few moments before taking a deep breath and exhaling. "I want you to see something, but first you have to be discharged from the hospital," she says as she walks out the door. I detest suspense and Bong-Cha's tenderness, which was incredibly irritating this time.

I'm baffled. I'm not sure what she's talking about right now. Because I'm not sure what's going on, my eyes widen and my eyebrows raises, leaving me speechless.

When Tae-Moon walks into the room, my heart beats faster beating with each step he takes closer. He is holding cherry blossoms. I believe he produced this adorable flower bouquet by himself. "How are you feeling, Moon?" he asks as he hands me the bouquet. Moon! I exclaim internally but don't show it, and then I say, "I'm good. Actually, I'm great."

"Well, I'm glad you're doing well," he says with a smile. His hands approach, and I allow him to get even closer. He takes my hand in his and tears up as he sees the needle in my hand. He is literally in tears. As his tears fall onto the hospital bed, he kisses my hands. "I'm afraid. I'm afraid of losing you, my moon."

"Shhh....." I say as he falls silent. Then he quickly wipes away his tears, and says, "I should go now. I don't want you to feel bad again. Get some rest. If you need anything, just call me," he says, smiling.

"Who's up next?" I ask. "Hyun-Bin," he says as he walks behind the closed door.

Unlike others, Hyun-Bin knows how to make me happy. He walks in with a bag of snacks, including my favourite chocolate, Ferrero Rocher. He didn't stay long; he simply gave me chocolate and kissed my forehead before departing. People are coming and going, and I haven't seen my parents in a long time. Maybe Bong didn't tell them.

My room is adorned and strewn with flower bouquets, get-well gifts, and balloons. It has been over a week since I regained consciousness, and Bong-Cha has still not shared what she said. My entire thought is focused on that thing. What will it be?

Bong-Cha walks into my room carrying a notebook. It appears to be the one that the man possesses.

She approaches and sits next to me, handing me the notebook "After the day you fainted, I went in search of the man. He is the librarian who promised to help me research the history of Silla. I saw him at the library and confronted him on your behalf. But I received nothing. All he said was, 'Give this to Aera and tell her I only have a little time.' He hands me the notebook and asks me to convey his regret for hurting you. I have already read this, but now you should read it by yourself," she says as she hands me the notebook and walks away. As she locks the door behind her, her expression becomes sorrowful

Part Two

Twenty One
Kim-Woo

I'm terrified to face the world alone. It is quite difficult for a child to live alone without the support of his or her parents. Now I find myself in this scenario, and everything I see is new to me. Everything is slowly dawning on me. I am gradually realizing that the universe I used to inhabit is no longer present. I should prepare to live independently.

The soldiers are escorting me somewhere inside. A massive arch seems to reach the boundless sky above me. Two soldiers are walking in front of me, escorting me to the empress, while two soldiers are walking behind me, carrying javelins. Javelins are large and sharp, and even a slight touch can result in cuts to your hands.

These weapons are nothing new to me; I'm accustomed to them. In fact, I played with a few and ended up cutting my hands.

I collide with the soldiers walking ahead of me, and then I notice that they came to a halt. All I can hear in the front is a majestic voice - the voice of the empress. When she speaks, the entire room falls silent. She's very cool!

"Kim-Woo, forward," the maid of honour says. As the voice approaches, I reluctantly step forward. I'm afraid they will abandon me at the orphan soldier's home. It is a facility for children who have lost both parents. Silla occasionally conquers other countries, and the numerous children from the conquered kingdom are trained here. This is known as 'The Blooming Warriors residence.' They teach children, turning boys into soldiers and girls into wonhwas.

Wonhwas are a type of Silla's female warriors. Silla is the only monarchy that utilizes the strength of women in combat. My mother is one of Silla's famous eight wonhwas. Other Wonhwa follow these eight superior wonhwas. My mother usually emphasizes that the true pride of Silla's struggle lies in the wonhwas. I'm not sure why she said that, but she meant it, and I agree. She is the most powerful woman I have ever seen. Everyone is captivated by her regal demeanour and striking eyes. She's always cool as she stretches her body and fires the arrow.

"All the kids here are like you. They'll treat you well." The maid of honour keeps making snide remarks about the facility and the children who live there. I despise socializing. I'm a quiet child who has spent my childhood in my parents' shadow. How can I interact with others?

Every step I take inside, however grudgingly, makes my heart race faster. It is common for children to feel anxious in such situations.

As I walk in, everyone inside is talking about me. "He's General Yoon-Woo's son," they exclaim. I'm not shocked that no one approached me to interact.

Because of my parents, I know they will keep their distance from me.

I am the son of the General of Silla. My father is General Yoon-Woo, and my mother, Eun-Soo, is one of the famous eight wonhwas. My father and mother met on the battlefield and married shortly after. After a few months, they had me. I am the only child from the royal family living in this orphan soldier's home.

My father was killed in a war. My mother then raised me on her own. My apologies, I lost her a few days ago. The rival kingdom of Silla launched an attack on the empress. The magnificent eight wonhwas are intended to defend the empress and my mother, who was a skilled archer. Unfortunately, she died in the conflict while protecting the queen from an arrow that was fired at her. She was stabbed in the lower neck, fought for a few minutes, and then died.

Death, sadness, and agony are all quite familiar to me. I didn't cry at my mother's death. Lastly, I wept over my father's death. That was the last time I cried. I haven't cried in over a year. I'm ashamed to be alive. Why should we struggle to live when we will all die one day? If death comes knocking on my door today, I'll gladly leave.

The maid of honour hands me some blue, dark blue garments. Then she provides some required items such as a pillow, blanket, and mat.

I walk inside and can't believe what I'm seeing. There are a lot of youngsters here, many more than I imagined. I go inside unwillingly, no one attempts to speak, and thank God for that. I dislike children, particularly girls.

"Where is my room?" I ask the guard standing near a pillar.

He bursts out laughing and declares, "There is no room. You should all sleep here. Girls on the left, males on the right."

I walk where his hands point, and all I see is a large empty hall with a half-sized wall and a wooden roof. There is nothing, just a few items like the pillow and blanket I'm using. "Where do I keep my things?" I ask, still stunned.

"There at the same place," he adds as he goes about his business.

I used to sleep in a bed made of lovely cotton, and my pillow was filled with swan feathers. I currently have the world's worst pillow and a rough blanket, and I don't even have a bed. Who knows, I might even lose this pillow and blanket.

I consider leaving my belongings in the sleeping hall. But I come to a halt after seeing her. I've never felt this way before. She is at the far end of the hall. It's a laundry facility, thus we should do our laundry ourselves.

The young lady is standing and directing others to do their laundry. She is dressed in a blue gown. The colour appears to be the same as the one I'm holding. She's also got a scarf on over her head. She tied it and pretended it was her long hair. What a fool I mutter under my breath as I walk down the hall.

It's nearly midday, and I haven't eaten anything since morning. I'm hungry, and my stomach is trembling. I would like to ask someone about their lunch schedule, but my ego prevents me from doing so. There's a battle going on between my ego and my hunger. They keep fighting, and eventually, my hunger prevails.

I approach the female, the hilarious one. "Hello," I say. With a terrible attitude, she turns around and says, "What?"

I mutter to myself, "I shouldn't talk to her," and inquire, "When do they provide lunch? I'm starving."

"We've already eaten," she says.

"What? When do they serve dinner?" I inquire.

"6:00 p.m.," she remarked, turning to resume her guiding duties.

I had never felt anything like this before. I'm not even aware of the sensation of hunger. Everything is unfamiliar to me. I'm hungry, and my mother isn't here to feed me. I start to gaze at the boundless empty sky. After my father died, I would often find solace in talking to the sky, envisioning the night sky as my father and cherishing his memory. Now that this blue boundless sky appears to be my mother, I begin conversing with it.

"Dear Mom, with whom do I discuss things we used to discuss? Who do I spend my evenings with when I'm not chatting to my father? Who will satisfy my hunger simply by gazing at me? Who do I sleep with if I'm afraid of the dark?" My head is filled with bewilderment, and the remorse inside me is caught in my throat, and I can feel the pain in my brain, which keeps beating my brain.

"Hey" Suddenly, a hand approaches me from behind. It's strange seeing that funny chick standing behind me. I have no idea why she is here. By arching my eyebrows, I conveyed my scepticism to her.

She hands me a half-eaten loaf of bread that still looks fresh and moist. It smells delicious. "What's this?" I'm curious.

"I brought this for you," she says, smiling. I despise girls, yet her smile is the loveliest thing I've seen today.

"No, I'm not hungry," I say emphatically. She laughs at me. "I know you're hungry," she adds as she takes my hand and sets the bread in my hands. "Look at your gaunt cheeks and sunken eyes; I can sense your hunger just by glancing at them." I'm utterly astonished. I'm not sure how, but she's driving me insane.

She is correct. I'm hungry, so I don't hesitate, and my ego has vanished, leaving only my hunger. I accept the bread she has offered and begin to eat. She turns around and begin going in the opposite direction.

When I take another bite, it gets stuck in my throat and causes a blockage. I get hiccups when I can't swallow or spit. I'm standing to get some water when I notice her approaching me with a tumbler of water. "I'm sorry, that's all I have," she adds as she hands me the water.

"That's fine," I answer. "My name is Kim-Woo," I explain.

"I know you're well-known around here. My name is Shin-Min," she introduces herself.

I give her a kind smile. What a lovely name! The ideal name for the ideal girl. She reminds me of the girls in my mother's bedtime stories; she has a princess-like heart. Mom, I've finally found someone who can understand my emotions just by looking into my eyes, just like you do.

Twenty Two
Kim-Woo

Days flew by like lightning, and with just a smidgeon of her, my entire existence became enchanting. I had no idea I was so attached to this girl. Because of her, I smile. She's the one who takes my hands in hers and shows me the wonders of existence. With the right people, life becomes lovely. And now I'm in the right place, with my family. I used to despise this facility, calling it the home for orphaned soldiers. I'm embarrassed by it. This place feels exactly like home. And it's no surprise that we're called blooming warriors; we deserve it. Our soldiers are exceptional in every situation. We excel as warriors, spies, and guards, and we are also remarkably attractive.

I came here when I was ten years old, and it has already been almost nearly ten years. Shin-Min is nineteen, and I turned twenty last month. She had matured well, and her skills had finally improved. I should mention her archery because this girl captivates me every time she stretches her shoulders before assuming her stance. Her aim is always as precise as her curves. Every time I see her, I am drawn in by her flexible physique.

We are moving to the palace today, and starting today, we will be serving as official soldiers and Wonhwas. My mother's spot among the great eight wonhwas has been left vacant since her death. And one of our wonhwa from our blossoming warrior's family will fulfil it today.

The palace appears beautiful, surrounded by massive gates and walls, and the craftsmen did an excellent job of decorating it. Our esteemed superiors are seated on the chairs positioned in front of the empress's throne, while the maids of honour are standing in all four corners of the palace. The throne is golden, and the dragon perched on the seat symbolizes the pride and courage of our kingdom. Two maids of honour standing on either side of the throne, and we are all assembled in the proper order. The wonhwas are on the right, while the troops are on the left. The seven superior wonhwas stand in front of the wonhwas. And our superiors are standing before us, with keen swords drawn.

"Here comes our honourable queen Kim-Jiso," the announcer says as the Empress approaches.

All other officials and maids of honour bow their heads and greet our queen, Kim-Jiso. The wonhwas salute by raising their bows to the heavens and saying, "Royal welcome from the Wonhwas." As troops, we draw our swords and raise them towards the sky, proclaiming,

"Royal welcome from the blossoming warriors." The gleam from our swords captures everyone's attention. The sword then moves to our chest to symbolize our loyalty, then downwards and back to the sword guard.

The empress approaches the throne and bows her head in respect for our country and our monarch. After she has settled down, the royal announcer begins the ceremony by inviting everyone. The superior warriors, as well as the senior wonhwas, then take their positions. The warriors and wonhwas call our names one by one, and we step up to accept our titles.

"Kim-Woo," my superior says as I step forward. I salute the queen and accept the scroll and sword. "From now on, Kim-Woo will serve as the general warrior of the blossoming warriors," she says as she hands me the sword.

"This sword is your pride, Kim-Woo; it belongs to your father, the renowned Yoon-Woo. Make him proud."

I return to where I was, and the wonhwa yells out, "Shin-Min." I haven't seen her since this morning, and when she comes forward, I can't take my gaze away from her. She looks stunning in the red and white dress. Her hair is pulled back, and she walks forward to salute the queen. The queen presents her with a scroll and a bow and arrow. The queen makes a motion and says, "Miss. Shin-Min will be a member of the renowned eight Wonhwas, and Eun-Soo's Bow and arrow will be handed to her as a mark of honor."

Shin-Min's eyes sparkled with delight, and she had not expected to be given such a title. She expands her body and makes a royal gesture when she receives the Archery kit. Oh, my poor heart. For her, it skips a beat.

I couldn't help myself, but all I could do was stare at her. The way her body moves as she fires the arrow. Everything about her, from the way she handles my mother's archery kit, draws me in. She appears attractive and graceful in this wonhwas dress, especially. Every time I see her, my heart tells me I don't deserve her. But I'm really smitten with this girl.

All I can think about is her. All of my memories revolve around her. She has been a part of my life since I was a child. All I do is fantasize about her, imagining what it would be like to be with her. I want to kiss her and tell her how much I adore her. I have been in love with her since the day we met, but all of my feelings for her have become stagnant. I'm worried about being rejected by her. That would be the worst feeling I've ever had.

The ceremony is coming to a finish. Later, I realized we must part for the time being. We have received our titles and must stay at the palace. We titled troops and wonhwas have separate residences within the palace and should not have any opportunity to meet until during wartime. What if I live my entire life without ever revealing my feelings? My face contorted, and I felt unhappy.

"Soldiers, disperse," the superior directs, and they march towards our residence. I am now a general, and I am in charge of all the aspiring fighters. I direct them all to form a separate line and follow me to our residence.

When I finally take a step straight away from where we had gathered, I look back to see her. She is flank by her Friends and the seven famous wonhwas. She returns my gaze, and our gazes lock. When I stop walking and fully turn to face her, she runs towards me. "I'm going to miss you," she adds as she gets closer. "I feel like I'm going to die because you're not here. I'd like to see you more often."

I freeze and stand still because I'm shy. My hands tremble as she embraces me even more tightly.

"Does she have feelings for me?" my mind keeps asking. I would like to express my feelings for her right now. But I'm still uncertain. She waves goodbye and dashes back.

My fellow soldiers and I return to our barracks after the ceremony. They gave us rooms. For the first time in a long time, we'll be sleeping in a room with four walls covered. My comrades are overjoyed to have accommodations. But there is only one room for four people.

They provided me with a separate room that had decent ventilation and enough space. There's a bed, so I kick the door open and run towards it. And when I did, I felt as though the bed was swallowing me whole. So soft and inviting. There is a sword hanger on the wall. I take the sword from the guard and lift it proudly. I feel powerful holding my father's sword in my hands. I don't want the sword to hang on the wall. My father used to say that a warrior's pride is his sword and that it should be treated with respect. So I'll have to hang it back up. That would be proper respect for the sword.

Twenty Three
Kim-Woo

When I ask my mother what love is, she replies, "When you love someone, they become a part of who you are. They'll be in the water you drink, your dreams, and the air you breathe. Love does not knock; it strikes. It hits you hard and reveals a different aspect of yourself. Everything you do will be different. You'll notice a different person within yourself, and that person will be the best version of you. Love perfects a person."

As I wake up from this dream, I let out a raspy breath and rub my eyes. Since the day my mother died, I haven't seen her in any of my dreams. It doesn't seem like a dream; it feels real. I wiped the sweat from my face and went for a walk to get some fresh air.

Some people admire the moon like for its allure objects and poetic qualities, poem, but for me, it represents my mother. When I see the infinite sky and the imperfectly perfect moon, I am reminded of my mother. I believe the sky is my father, and the moon is my mother, and they love each other even when they are not together.

My gaze falls at Wonhwa's residence while admiring the moon. It's not far; it's just across the walkway. However, we are not permitted to enter because it is a women's residence. My gaze wanders aimlessly over that building, hoping to see Shin-Min emerge as I did. But she is nowhere to be found.

Only I miss her. Perhaps she's peacefully resting in her bed, dreaming of someone else or a prince who will come and rescue this enchanting girl.

"How can I accept that she is sleeping without even thinking about me?" My head flips out.

"Hello, Kim-Woo! I'm sorry, General Kim," Ban-Ru says as he approaches me.

"Hey man, just call me Kim-Woo," I say, tapping his shoulder.

"OK, why are you here?" his large eyes point to where I am standing. I don't want to lie because he's my friend, and who else should I share my feelings with if not him?

"I miss her," I murmur, lowering my gaze.

"Shin-Min?"

"I think I love her," my cheeks flush, my eyes narrow, and my lips pursed. I'm completely crimson.

"You should confess then," he simply says. I'm terrified of being rejected by her. "What if she neglects my feelings? What if she declines?" I ask.

"Rejection is preferable to unexpressed emotions. If she rejects you, at least you'll have a reason to move on," he says. I come to a halt, and silence replaces our conversation.

"I can assist you with this," he says, breaking the silence.

"Really?" I ask, my eyes wide.

"Yep," he says.

"So, what should I do now?" I sound foolish.

"Invite her to a private place and confess," he suggests. I'm eager to talk to her, but this fool suggests that we should meet in secret.

"Private! No, man, I'm terrified of her," I exclaim.

"If she rejects you, it will remain confidential between the two of you, ensuring that no one else will be aware. That's why I suggest meeting with her privately." He seems to be quite intelligent.

"That's a fantastic idea, thank you," I remark as I walk inside.

I keep replaying the scene in my head. I lean against the bed, rehearsing what to say or how to confess.

The next morning, I wake up earlier and make my way to the training location. I have been looking for her since six o'clock in the morning. My junior warriors have started to arrive, but she has not arrived yet. Perhaps she is eating her breakfast. I cross my legs and wait for her, gripping my sword tightly.

Time passes, and she finally enters. My girl, I mutter under my breath and stand up from where I'm seated.

Soldiers and wonhwas are training in the same field, yet they are separated by a significant distance. She is at the

North Pole, while I am at the South Pole. I can barely see her because we are so far apart. She begins to shoot the arrows, and none of them miss. Every time she releases an arrow, it feels as though she's piercing my tender heart.

"Shin-Min," I am rushing through things like a moron. I can tell from her expression that she is clueless. "Are you going to annoy me here, too?" she asks as I reach over to her.

"What?" I come to a standstill. I expected her to grin at me, give me a big hug, and tell me she missed me, but she did the opposite. "I have something to say,' I say.

"Alright," she says, remaining silent to allow me to speak, but I don't say anything. "I'd like to talk privately. Can we meet in the mountains?" I inquire. Her eyes widen and she exclaims,

"What? No way. I never skip training."

"How about the evening?" I suggest. "That sounds convenient," she remarks. "I'll see you there," I grin at her, widening my mouth to show off all of my teeth. I returned to my training location. I'm still waiting for the evening to arrive, and my friends are laughing at me. And the thought of seeing her makes my heart race.

After taking a quick shower, I leave our room. I dash there on my horse, but when I go to retrieve my horse, I couldn't find Shin's horse. So, I'll have to move quickly.

The sky turns orange, and it is as if like the sun sinking into the vastness of the sky merging with it. The breeze brushes against my skin, giving me goose bumps. I'm almost there, and as I get closer, I notice my girlfriend standing under the trees, her face sparkling in the sunlight. The radiant smile that spreads across her face causes me to lose control.

I dismount from the horse and approach her on foot. My steps are short and my breathing is shallow, and she approaches me when she senses my hesitation. The ache spreads across my ribcage as oxygen becomes trapped inside my lungs. I'm having trouble breathing. My breath finally came out after a long, laboured effort and rasp.

Her cherry lips make me feel wild. When I kiss her, how does she taste? What does her skin look like when the sun shines on it? And how does she moan when I'm on top of her? "Don't think anything crazy___ Kim-Woo," I murmur under my breath as I try to keep my cool.

"What is the reason for your silence? What do you want to talk about?" she inquires.

"Come closer," I say, sounding strange. She's anxious and sweating, so I pull her close and wipe away her perspiration before saying, "I'm in love," in a low and husky voice.

I can feel her shivering. My arms wrapped around her torso, and all she did is remain silent. Her silence diverts my attention from something chaotic yet intriguing. I gently push her hair behind her ears and playfully tug it, causing my breath to tickle her. My breath envelops her, and all she can do is moan. She approaches to kiss, but I kiss her first. Our kiss becomes more passionate and intense. As I kissed her passionately, my hands slides under her clothes.

She suddenly pushes me and takes off running. I race after her and yell, "What's wrong?" when she comes to a standstill.

"I thought you love me, but your thoughts are out of control. I'm not the girl you're looking for," she yells back, and the words pierce me deeply. I get closer, and she starts shaking.

"Hey Shin, my intentions are not lustful," I say as I gently touched her head. "I'm madly in love with you. I really like you. I love you with all my heart, and I promise that I won't touch you again without your permission," as she rushes up to me and hugs me. Her eyes are welling up with tears, and I know she's hesitant to say anything, but she'll confess when she feels safe.

I hug her back, and as our bodies make contact, she says, "Hold me in your arms and watch me break into a thousand petals of love," and plants a kiss on my cheek.

Twenty Four
Kim-Woo

Our love tale has become extremely popular among the people of our homeland, and people are still talking about it. They are anxiously awaiting our marriage, but we are not prepared for it. Before I embark on any serious affairs, I'd like to contribute something to my kingdom. My homeland has given me the pride and honour I have today, and I cannot simply settle for marriage and live a simple life as a Normie. I want people to remember my story of bravery in the future.

I miss her so much that all I can do is think about her. She completely captivated me, and I can't get her thoughts out of my head. I haven't seen or heard from her in a week. It's awful without her. Every day when our food is delivered, I anticipate her arrival, but she never comes. We got into a disagreement, and I yelled at her. That was a tremendous error, and before I could apologize, the empress assigned me and my fellow troops to protect all four borders. Our kingdom is under siege. Our rival nation, Goguryeo, could invade us. They have already attempted to enter our realm surreptitiously from the south side, but our troops have successfully defended against them, and security measures are now tight.

When I hear the sound of hooves approaching, I inform all of our warriors and tell them to prepare their swords. But then I hear the sound of a horse approaching from behind, and I instantly recognize whose horse it is: it's my girl, Shin. I'm delighted she's coming. At least I'll get a chance to apologize and console her today. When she lands and ties her horse to the side, she turns away from me. I know she's mad at me, but I wasn't expecting her to ignore me. We typically argue and patch up within hours, but this one has been going on for a week or more.

"Hey Shin," I say, drawing her hand closer to mine. She's so firm and hasn't moved; perhaps she's aware of my actions. She's my girl, and she knows everything about me.

After giving me the food and the scroll from Queen, she didn't even stay for a moment and didn't give any chance for me. She begins to walk over to untie her horse, then climbs on and rides. What? No, I would like to apologize. I ask my fellow soldiers to keep watch over the boundaries while I quickly go to fetch my horse.

I spot a few horse steps in the mud and ride faster in this direction until I approach the woods and find her. She is slowly walking the horse, and she is unhappy and upset, and it is all because of me. I approach her cautiously, dismount, and begin strolling with my horse behind her. She comes to a halt and stares back at me. No one can guess Shin's actions and her mind-set. So I approach her gently. Shin is standing behind a tree with her horse, and I approach her gently, leaving my horse behind.

She isn't facing me; all I see is her massive and sexy ass, and when I hold her hands, she swings and turns, her sword pressed against my throat. Any slight movement on my part could result in my throat being sliced in half. I stood still and I am not moving; I swallowed, and my throat made a slight movement, causing the sword to make a small cut, I just get a little hurt and there was no bleeding.

"Enough," she says as she lowers the sword, "don't justify yourself." I'm a moron; I should have done what she asked me to do before this fight. All of this conflict is due to me.

"I'm sorry, let me apologize Shin," I say as my hands slide up her arms and settle on her shoulders. She feels me, she feels my touch, and she softens. "I asked you to marry me, but you turned me down, and it hurts. Do you remember what you said that day?" she cries, her voice deep and terrible, and when it reaches my ears, I am overwhelmed with guilt.

I met Shin in the woods before our kingdom was attacked by Goguryeo. "I want to do something for this kingdom," I remarked when she asked me to marry her. "And I'm afraid I can't marry you right now. If we marry, you will become my responsibility, something I cannot accept. Shin, please realize that I want to accomplish something that future generations will remember. Please." I said.

"I can understand your desire to contribute something to our country and Silla's history, but what if I lose you in the war?" she murmured as she grasped my hands in hers. "We all know our kingdom is in trouble, and I know there will be a major war soon, but I want to die as your wife. At the very least, I'd like to be yours for a single day. That's all I need."

"Look, I'm not going to die; I promise I'll come for you after this war," I said, kissing her.

"What if I die?" She didn't stop kissing. She closed her eyes and cried. She said again, "What if I die before you? Please, at least let us have sex. I'd like to be yours for today."

I released her grip, took a step away from her, and yelled, "No, I don't want sex that would be a distraction. I don't want anything to distract me, not even you." I turned and walked away. I recall every conversation we had, and I nearly killed her that day. I'm embarrassed by my self-centred behaviour.

"I'm sorry, Shin, please," I say, grasping her legs and begging her to forgive me. After a few minutes, she begins to cry, and her tears fall on my face. "I love you," she says as I turn my head to face her.

I proceed to kiss her on the thighs. Then she takes a seat next to me carefully. I start kissing; it has been a week since our last kiss, so my kisses are intense and burning. Actually, I'm not kissing, but eating my girl. I gently move towards her neck after showering her all over her face, and when I land my first kiss on her neck, she moans, which is my favourite sound. Raspy and adorable.

Her touch falls off my cheek, and soon she falls unconscious on me, "Hey Shin" I tap her face, and her eyes twitch, but she falls unconscious every time. She can't hear what I'm saying. My emotions are overwhelming because I can't wake her up no matter how hard I try. Her body temperature is gradually dropping, and she is becoming cold. "No, you should stay conscious, shin."

Fear arises between my ribs and spreads throughout my body, and I am unable to think. My heart, lungs, and brain are all shattered by the pain. I grab her, raise her in my hands, and carry her to Wonhwa's residence. I didn't think twice about it and went up to Shin's room, where the other girl was sitting on her bed. They are actually roommates. When I enter, it startles her companion as I lift Shin unconscious. "What happened?" she screams, terrified. "She fainted on the way, so I'm bringing her here," I explain as I approach Shin's bed.

"I told her not to come in this situation, but she came for you," she says as I pull the blanket over my shin and settle next to her. "Is she ill?" I do not know. "She's on her period," she says before going silent.

"Can you bring some food up?" I requested to her. She goes down to bring food, and as she does so, I try to wake shin. Shin does not become conscious. I splash some water on her face, but there is no reaction. I repeated it once, twice, and three times, and on the fourth attempt, she moved her eyeballs and tried to open her eyelids. However, she couldn't because they were stuck. Slowly, she opens her eyes, and all she does is hold me. I can see the unmistakable anxiety in her eyes, which is all about the war and her fear of losing me.

"I'm not leaving you, and I'm not going anywhere. I'll spend the night with you," I say as I stroke her hair. I lift her face in my hands and place her hands on my waist before planting a gentle kiss on her forehead. I can feel the warmth radiating from her as I do so. Her friend arrives with food, and she smiles at me.

Twenty Five
Kim-Woo

Blood spilled all over the place, and all I see is red, no, blood. Everything is over. This conflict has claimed many lives, and numerous individuals have lost their fathers, sons, daughters, and other family members who fought in this war.

There are dark rivulets running along the ground, and there is an excessive amount of blood. Therefore, I proceed to the area where someone may require help. I notice Ban-Ru on the ground, torn between life and death. A knife stabbed him in the lower chest, and he is bleeding profusely. I yell for the soldiers to come and rescue him, and they comply.

Almost half of my fellow soldiers had died, and only a few of us survived. The conflict ended, and we were on the verge of losing the battle. Our soldiers evacuated our empress to the safest part of our palace, while all the wonhwas and soldiers continued to fight until our blooming soldiers made a strategic manoeuvre, and I successfully decapitated the king with my sword. His blood soaked my blade, streamed all over the ground, and splashed on me. The soldiers fled in fear after their monarch's death.

Then we informed our empress, who dispatched the fortress guards to rescue the injured warriors.

My gaze searches for Shin, but she is nowhere to be found. I'm terrified on the inside, and I rush to inspect her all over the battlefield. During this intense battle, numerous female warriors were killed. Every time I see a deceased woman on the ground, my heart sinks. "Shin, where are you?" I yell, dashing about, searching for her.

"Kim-Woo," calls out from the north side of the battleground. As I make my way over there and see my girl standing on the sandy field. I can't see anything clear because the air is so polluted.

When I approach closer, I discover she has arrows lodged in her right chest. I clutch her in my hands, and she's bleeding.

When she gets close to me and I try to lift her, blood splashes from her mouth and she gasps for air. Suddenly, her eyes were wide, and she didn't let go of the oxygen she had taken in. Then I discover blood streaming from my mouth, and then I realized an immense pain in my stomach. It's a javelin, it travels from Shin's abdomen, and she gradually loses consciousness. I took the Javelin away from myself, and I can't take it away from her because she'll die if I do.

We collapse onto the ground, fighting for our lives. I take Shin's hand in mine; she is already drowsy. "My love," I whisper, my voice half-lost, swallowing the rest inside. "Shin, please stay with me," my eyes welled up with tears. I thought I would never cry for anyone in my life, but she made me cry.

Her eyes squint shut, and she murmurs, "I'm sorry, Kim-Woo." Her breath is scratchy, and she's on the verge of death, and I'm bleeding as well.

I'm crying, holding her in my arms, feeling the weight of all my mistakes as she barely opens her eyes. All she ever asked of me was to marry, and I'm fucking guilty that I didn't even fulfil her request.

"Sometimes I wish you understood me," she says, waving her hands asking me to come closer,

"You're really self-centred. I believed you would care about me at some point, but you do not know how much I despise this general Kim-Woo, I wish to meet you again; I want you to adore me as if I am your burning desire; I want you to chase after me and lavish all of your affection on me. I love you with all my heart, and I want you to come look for me if we have another life." Her eyes close and she falls silent.

"Shin, I promise I'll come in search of you and make you realize my unconditional love," I say as the love of my life dies in my hands. As I gradually close my eyes, I notice soldiers approaching us from a distance.

Twenty Six
Aera

I don't like how I forgot your voice, I don't like how the memory of you smiling at me faded away. I don't like how I didn't recognize the love of my life. Every time you try to make me remember our memory I end up disappointing you. I'm ashamed of myself for making you embarrassed when you try to confess. Why can't I just recognize you by just looking into your eyes? I even got thousands of memories of us and I didn't even give a try to remember you, I just thought it's all my nightmares.

Now I understand everything the fortune teller said, she asked me to wake up and it's from the coma and the pencil she hands is to note down my perspective of our past, All the things are relating and I finally realize, I'm Shin-Min.

When I finished reading the notebook, I scream. The way he described our story hurts me; he doesn't know my perspective on it, and I wish he did. "What happened?" When I scream in remorse, Bong-Cha appears. "I'm the one on the painting. It's him and I." I'm sobbing, my agony has turned to grief and has fallen from my eyes, and my eyes have turned red from despair.

"Please help me. Bong-Cha, I'm at a loss for what to do." I'm blubbering, my heart is racing, and my breathing is becoming shallow. I can't exhale, and it feels like all of my organs have stopped working.

"Breathe it's okay. You'll be just fine. Just take a deep breath. Remind yourself of all the time you spent with him in the past. He's still yours, and you still have an opportunity to win his heart. Trust this struggle is part of the process. And believe that as long as you don't give up, no matter how dismal things appear to be, you will succeed."

"But, I'm scared," I say, quivering my lower lips. My voice is trembling uncontrollably.

"I already read the book while you were in the hospital, and I know how much he loved and loves you. Don't worry, he's just your man, right?" she claims.

I get out of bed without thinking about how I look, grab my phone and my bag, and dash out of the home. It's freezing out, and I'm dressed in my nightgown, waiting for a cab. I wait about an hour and get no cab. So I dash to the park where we typically meet. The park was closed, and there are no people in sight. Oh, oh, where am I going to find him? I'm crying, wiping my eyes with my sleeve, and standing like an idiot. People are staring at me as though I'm nuts.

Later, I recall the museum, and I should go check it out. I sprint to the museum since I don't want to wait for a cab. I am short on time. I should get there as quickly as possible. The sky begins to pour, and shit time makes everything worse. I'm sprinting there in a nightgown and slippers I used to wear inside the house.

I couldn't run because the thunder and lightning gives me a migraine, so I give up and fell on the pavement. I'm completely saturated, and my vision is blurring. My hair falls on my face and covers nearly half of it. I appear pitiful.

I muster enough bravery to resume my sprint to the museum. As I run, the rain begins to slow and turn to mist. And when the mist falls on my skin, I remember what he told me about losing his memories and writing down what he doesn't want to forget in a notebook. I should've read this notebook earlier. I shouldn't have let things go this bad.

My hair and clothes cling to my body, revealing my inner, and I'm trembling from the cold. I sprint to the museum, tucking my hair behind my ears. I arrive at the museum after a forty-minute run and a few slips.

When I walk in, the museum curator stares at me and orders me to leave. I'm at a loss as to why he's doing this. Later, I realize I resemble a destitute brat. Then I slowly approach him and say, "Uncle, look at me. I'm Aera. I'm coming here more frequently. You remember?"

He's taken aback; he's used to seeing me well-dressed and with a cute demeanor, "Is that you? Are you all right?" he asks.

"I'm perfectly fine. I'd like to get in right away. So I dashed all the way here. May I go now?" I ask. "You ran all the way?" He looks up and down a few times before asking me to wait. Later, he comes up to me with a jacket and presents it to me, saying, "Your clothes are transparent because of the rain, have this."

"Thank you very much," I reply as I enter the museum.

I head to the art gallery as soon as I walk in to look for him. I see a sword on my walk to the gallery; it's his sword. The museum displayed it and referred to him by name. Finally, he got what he wished for, he's a part of Korean history. I'm happy and proud of him. I walk into the art section and no one is there. My eyes begin to flood up once more. Fear develops in my ribs, my throat becomes blocked, and I am unable to speak or breathe. All I can do is cry. As I cry, no voice comes out.

"I'm afraid of losing you again," I sob in front of the painting. "I'm worried I'll wake up one day and have no memory of you. Most of all, I'm afraid you'll abandon me again and abandon me to my overwhelming misery. Please, just once, I'd like to see you and tell you how I feel about you." I gather my strength and let out the voice of my tears. It's awful to feel this way. Only love has the ability to make you both joyful and sad.

"Shin_____" I turn around and stare at him; the way he refers to me gives me Goose bumps.

He spreads his arms wide and motions for me to hug him. I rush over to hug him. When I touch him, I feel the same way I did before, warm and safe. He wipes my tears away and tells me, "Don't cry, you deserve smiles."

"I'm sorry"

"For what?"

"You are the person who walked into my life and made me feel the world in a different way. I'm sorry for everything I did. I adored you and continue to admire you every time we're together. I was abused as a youngster, and the queen took me into the home. As a result, I detested males. I used to despise males until I met you. Remember, I'm disappointed in you, but it doesn't mean I despise you. I really want you to be a part of my life." I take his hands in mine and kiss him.

"I know you love me with all your heart; you've made me a hopeless romantic." He says and I smile as my eyes well up with tears of love.

"Finally, you did it, you got what you wanted. I saw your sword here, and you're part of Korean history," I explain.

"No. Life taught me that you are the cause of my existence. When you died in my arms, the agony killed me as well. Then I realized that it is only your unconditional love that matters, not pride and courage."

I'm proud of him, and his mother will be as well. When I witnessed him say all of these things, my heart springs inside my chest with joy. Finally, I understand the genuine meaning of love; the feeling that I have when I'm with him is what love feels like.

When he says, "It's time for me to let go of you," all of my delight vanishes.

"What? Why?

I_____ can't comprehend"

"We can't live together," he says.

"Is that because of our age? People are happy despite a large age difference, and it's the twenty-first century, age doesn't matter, just love does," I yell at him. "It's not about my age, it's about me Shin," he says quietly.

"What's the matter with you? Are you married?" I inquire, my voice quiet.

He closes his eyes for about a minute and declares, "I'm not alive." "Stop making fun of it; how can this happen? You're kidding me right?" I smile, one of the bitterest smile I ever did.

I suddenly recognize him in his previous appearance. His appearance shifts from the way he was previously to that of a young soldier. No way, this isn't true. What's the matter with my eyes? I have no idea.

"This is the truth; you must accept it," he replies, returning to his previous expression.

"No___" I shout.

"How did my mother and friends perceive you?" I ask. My heart is expecting him to declare that everything is a joke and to ask if I want to marry him.

"I remember everything about my past when I was nineteen, and since then I've been looking for you.

Then I discovered that you had not yet been born. So I waited for you to reincarnate. Unfortunately, I died when I was twenty-one years old. I realize I can't live any longer, so I keep looking for you as a soul."

"What?" I say that with a heavy heart.

"Yeah, I'm your imaginary friend, remember?" he replies as I recall my imaginary childhood friend.

"I've been trying to make you remember our past since you were a child. But, after a certain age, I noticed you become dissatisfied with my engagement. So I've decided to approach you when you're older. I followed you everywhere you went. I worked so hard to make you remember our story and love."

Everything he says is correct, and I can relate to it now. But my heart continues to reject the truth. It's difficult for me to see him as a soul in front of me.

"Why did you make me remember everything if you were going to leave again?" I inquire in hushed tones, the rest of my voice goes inside.

"That's why I reincarnated, Shin. I'd like to prove to you, my sincere unconditional love. That's why I'm keeping this tight in this world without going to the afterlife." He repeats this as his vision flickers and he fades away.

"No__

Wait, please,"

I scream. I hurry forward and embrace him tightly in my arms, determined not to let him go. He continues to add, "I'm sorry I can't make it in this birth, too." "Don't be sorry, I promise, I'll come to find you if we have another life," I say this as his soul shatters into cherry petals on my fingertips. A little petal falls on my hands, and I tighten my grip, refusing to let the petal go.

My father usually claims that I have a relationship with cherry blossoms, and today I realized what he means.

Twenty Seven
Bong-Cha

He learned from whatever he did, and everything he encountered along the way, and he accepted it with grace. He had taught her another extremely crucial life lesson by dying.

Days passed he had gone. She misses him, his laughter and voice, their long quiet eye contact, and his company. But she had the distinct impression that he is someplace nearby, doing his own thing and offering his affection, just as he did when they were together.

I push the door inside and open the door to give food to Aera. After that day she locked herself inside her room and didn't allow anyone in, except me and Tae-Moon. He's the therapy for her trauma. But, still, she couldn't imagine herself falling in love or getting married.

"I cooked your favorite Gimpab, have some," I say as her gaze is distracted from something she's holding.

"Not in the mood to eat," she added, dismissing the meal and returning her gaze to the object in her hands.

"What's that?" I enquire as I take her hand in mine to examine her. "It's him," she replies, her eyes welling up. "Him?" What she's saying perplexes me. I have no idea what transpired that day at the museum. He's a soul, she remarked, and it's difficult for her to let go of him.

"That day," she begins, and I let her finish with a mute reaction. "When I saw him that day, he said I deserve smiles, but how can I smile without him? Why can't we be together even in our rebirth?" tears fall and she turns red. She lifts her hands and closes her eyes for a few minutes. I give her a cloth to clean her face, she sneezes and wipes her tears off.

"I saw him in my dreams last night. Like always, my dreams of him are peripheral, I was holding him in my arms and this time I didn't let him go, I made him stay with me. Then I woke up and realized it was all a dream." She falls silent once more.

"Do you know how it feels to be unable to recall the voice of your love? It's bad, I swear. I'm terrified. Bong-Cha, his memories are fading away from me, and I'm afraid of completely forgetting him," she stabs her nail into her skin, injuring herself.

"Can you show me what's on your palm?" She grasps something and wraps her palms around it tightly.

"That's him. He shattered into cherry petals, and this is all I have, the only thing he left for me. It's a part of him." She continues to speak, and all of her regrets are falling as words. She'll feel better if she shares.

"I want you to give it to me," she doubtfully looks at me and is hesitant to give the petal to me. "You can trust me, Aera," I say and she hands the petal to me. I approach my room on the next second she gave me the petal.

I return after an hour, and when I open the door to her room, I discover she finished half of the meal I brought for her. I grin at her, but she's a jerk. I close the door behind me and approach her, saying, "Show your hand," but she has no idea what I'm talking about. She reluctantly opens her palms, and as I place the object I made, she sobs.

Because I'm good at art and enjoy making miniatures, I placed the petal inside a pendant I made and filled it with resin to make it permanent.

Aera is charming, and she hugs me while wearing the chain. "Now he'll be with you forever," I remark as I kiss her on the cheek. I let her slumber for a while offering her a notebook to record her memories of him. I put her to bed and cover her with her quilt. When I leave I decide to leave the door open.

Aera wakes up excited the next morning. Dalia and I are really in disbelief as she prepares to go to college. I help her gather her belongings while Dalia cleans her room.

"I can't lock him inside the small room," Aera says as she joins me on the couch. "I'm going to have fun in this world with him." I'm not sure to whom she's referring. "Who? Tae___?" As I begin, I notice the chain around her neck. She has it on and when she hears the 'who' from me, she gestures and touches the pendant.

I'm glad I didn't continued the phrase.

I get a call from Tae-Moon, so I go outside to discuss. "Hello," I say. He didn't even acknowledged my 'hello'. All he wants to know about is Aera and her health, whether she has food, and so on._____

"She's fine, she's fine. She'll attend college today." "Really?" I can tell by his voice that he's bouncing with excitement.

"May I ask you a question?" When I say this, he falls silent and answers, "Sure."

"We're all aware that Aera will not love you. She can't take him out of her heart, and you can't take his place. Then why are you doing such things? Sorry if this offends you, but this is the reality."

"I'm well aware of this; whenever I approach her, she says she belongs to someone else, and sometimes I feel the same way, that I don't own her. She belongs to someone else."

"How come? Why are you torturing yourself?"

"I know she belongs to someone else, but my pitiful heart is not accepting it. It is she. She's the one I want to see before bed and after I get up. And I swear I've never been more certain about anyone or anything in my life. It's her, and I know it without a doubt." His voice becomes deeper, and he swallows half of what he had uttered.

"No, you should give up on her"

"I'm never going to give up on her. Because giving up on her is like losing a piece of myself," he states emphatically. I'm at a loss for words. I'm curious about his unstated feelings towards Aera. I fall silent.

"Hello? Are you there?" His voice interrupts my silence.

"Do you want me to pick you guys up? I want to make sure she's okay, and I don't want her to walk to college. She'll be fatigued after going through so much. May I, then?" He inquires tenderly, his voice calm and pleasant.

"I don't think it's a good idea. Aera had affection for you before she knew her past, and spending time with you or receiving favors from you will be awkward for her. I hope you get it," I say.

"Fine, just seeing her doing well is enough for me. See you later, let's meet at college," he says as he hangs up the phone.

The most basic element of love is not to fall in love but to be genuinely loved by another, to know a love that comes out of reason and decision rather than impulse. Aera needs to be loved by someone who chooses to love her; in this situation, Kim-Woo and Tae-moon are the same.

Everything changed but one didn't, our punctuality. We rush to catch the bus as usually. Aera, Dalia and me are running and finally we board in.

Epilogue
Kim-Woo

My soul reunited in a location filled with emptiness after I crested there. There's nothing here but a large silence and a moving sky filled with stars. Because the stars are sleeping, they take a snooze on this pitch. It's like being stranded in the middle of the ocean. I can't see anything, there's no coastline, and no place to go. It's as though I'm moving along with the infinite sky and this empty landscape.

I keep pleading for a chance to see my girl one last time.

But if I can't move, how can I return to see her? I really want to go back and convey something. Please, God, have mercy. Just one last time.

Suddenly, the sky turns blue. It gradually changes colourful and then transforms into a beautiful blue sky. I can see the sky moving, and as I glance down, I see my soul standing on the bridge, which leads to Aera's institution.

I rush back to see her, then realize I can't move. I'm locked here, and all I can do is wait for Aera to arrive. I can hear her footsteps approaching from afar.

I give her a smile and wave my hands in the air. But she didn't notice me, so I wondered, "Am I invisible?" Her heartbeat is so loud that I can hear it as she gets closer. Then I notice this petal chain around her neck. When

I shattered, she took it with her. My eyes well up with tears, yet a soul cannot cry.

On the way she passes through me and our path crosses. As she goes, our appearances gradually changed. My look changed to that of a soldier, and hers to that of a wonhwa. When we meet, she returns her gaze to me and grins. I know she can't see me, but she can feel my presence now.

She comes to a halt, and her friends inquire as to why she is standing there. "He's here," she says. "I need a few moments." Her friends understand her feelings and allow her to spend time with me.

"People says, effort matters than a milestone and you made a lot of efforts to make me realize your love. I adore you wholeheartedly. You'll be here indefinitely." She touches her pendant, which is hanging around her neck and falls just above her chest.

"I want you to keep something in mind. Know that no matter what comes our way, I will always love you. You gave me a feeling that no one else had ever given me. We are the epitome of perfection in my opinion. You have the power to make everything okay even if it isn't. I might be anywhere in the world, but as long as you're mine, I'll make it happen. I know I'll be fine without you, but I don't think I'll be happy. I hope that our bond of affection never changes. We've become entwined, yours and mine. I'm yours and I'll definitely find you." When she delivers the last statement, she says it with all her heart and her voice shakes. She begins walking and after a little further, she disappears from my sight.

"Knowing and loving you is one of the greatest gifts I've ever received. Even I'm dead my soul always chases you," when the sky darkened again, my soul shattered and entered the realm of the afterlife.

About the Author

Gulsar Almash

Gulsar Almash an aspiring young author from Tamil Nadu. From her childhood, she visualizes something big in the sense of reaching people through her inking. After spending years reading books and consuming them, she finally decides to narrate her own book. Gulsar lives with her mother and two crazy sisters. She values her love, family, friends, and faith more than anything else. You almost always find her engaged in a book if she isn't with her friends.

Instagram: gulsar_almash

www.ingramcontent.com/pod-product-compliance
Lightning Source LLC
LaVergne TN
LVHW041709070526
838199LV00045B/1266